LEON M A EDWARDS

COLD **BONES**

Narwick

COLD BONES

www.leonmaedwards.com

JOIN MY LEON M A EDWARDS CLUB

Leon M A Edwards Club members get free books, ahead of publications. So you can enjoy the book and form an opinion of how it made you feel.

Members only get emails about any promotions and when the next book is ready for receiving.

See the back of the book for details on how to sign up.

COLD BONES

LEON M A EDWARDS

I would like to dedicate this book to Andrea, Alina and Lilia for leaving me to it, to write.

I would also like to dedicate this book to my dad who passed away on Monday 25th January 2021. He will be sorely missed by his five children, eight grandchildren and a loving wife.

ACKNOWLEDGMENTS

Thank God for giving me the confidence to start writing and the ability to write a story.

SEQUENCE OF EVENTS

November 2020

THERE IS a small town called Marion in North Carolina, a quiet leafy town in McDowell County.

Here, in this family-orientated town where everyone knows each other, nothing exciting ever happens. The only crime that takes place is people dropping litter on the sidewalk. You can leave your front door unlocked and you do not have to worry about being robbed. Everyone knows each other's business and news travels fast. Nothing can be kept a secret in this place.

THE TOWN HAS a population of around 7,891 people. The average family take-home salary is $35,463.

Marion stands at the edge of the Blue Ridge Mountains, just off Interstate 40. The views of the mountains are amazing.

THE MARION POLICE DEPARTMENT is made up of a sheriff, a chief, four investigators and a lieutenant with four squads of police officers.

The department handles interviews and interrogations, sexual assault investigation, crime scene investigations, and financial crimes.

THE LOCAL SHERIFF is friendly and approachable. He attends community meetings on menial problems like noise pollution from neighbours' houses, beer bottles left lying around and residents not parking responsibly in their road. He has been working in Marion for the past five years.

He began working here in early 1982 and had never experienced any homicide cases. His main caseload consisted of settling small disputes amongst neighbours.

He routinely goes to his regular diner round the corner from the police station; such is his routine that you could set your watch by him.

THE ONLY REAL crime that has happened in this fair town was when a boy went missing in 1982. No one knows what happened to him and this has been an unsolved case for Marion's police department ever since.

They found a suspect who they charged with his disappearance because they found an item of clothing in his possession. He had a cap which the boy's parents identified as belonging to their child. The cap had blood on the edge of the visor. There were no other items in the man's possession.

The man could not explain how it had shown up in his accommodation. He swears that he did not know of the boy and that he had an alibi. However, he could not tell them where he had been on the day of the disappearance.

He has kept his alibi a secret ever since.

EVEN THOUGH THE body had not been discovered, the police still arrested him for possession of the cap. Back then, in 1982, there was not a lot of evidence needed to convict a person. If this case came up today, he would not have been held. Yet, at the same time, he refused to give his alibi.

THE MAN WORKED as a casual labourer on a farm with the intention of only staying in Marion for a few days. He then had plans to move on and eventually settle in Los Angeles where he would study to be a doctor.

He came into town in the late summer of 1982 and helped with the harvesting. He kept to himself and never went into town to sample the restaurants or bars. He used the money he earned to help towards his first year of medical school.

THE BOY who disappeared lived in a quiet road called 'Yancey Road', which is in a nice area of Marion. He was a regular six-year-old child who never gave trouble, not even to the police. No one expected a child like him to go missing as he had regular friends who never got into trouble. He hung around with three other kids in a wood not far from their residence. They did not stray far.

His name was Daniel Harris and he had fair skin and straw-coloured hair that sat on his head like a mop. He had an inquisitive mind and enjoyed exploring new things. He also saw himself as a little bit of a detective, always trying to find something out of the ordinary.

His parents have kept his bedroom the same since he disappeared. One of the things he has on his desk is a child's detective book.

The hardest thing they found was not being able to have closure and even though the town moved on, they stayed in 1982. The world around them changed with time but their house has not, and you can feel it is in the past.

His parents smile on the outside and enjoy life, but they feel the same original pain from all those years ago.

His father is a fireman, and his mother works in a boutique shop.

DANIEL'S FRIENDS were William Jackson, Bill Walker and Jack Hall; they are all aged 43 now.

William is African American, short, with a slight paunch from enjoying his food a bit too much. His afro hair is cut quite short. His face is clean-shaven, and he has aged well. He wears dark brown trousers with a mustard shirt and brown tie. He is an accountant and has two kids of his own aged four and six. His father is a farm worker, and his mother is a nurse.

Bill is Caucasian, tall and skinny and looks like he is under-nourished. His black hair is short and scraggly, and his poor attempt at a beard is quite patchy. He wears faded grey jeans with a black sweat jumper and worn-out brown suede shoes. He has not done much with his life and is a bit of a drifter. He does casual labour in and around Marion. He never married and does not have a girlfriend. His father is a car mechanic, and his mother is a waitress. His parents still live in Marion in the same house. He finds the past is too difficult for him to stay in Marion. He has a slight drug problem and comes and goes in Marion to remember his friend. He feels some kind of guilt about when Daniel disappeared.

Jack is Caucasian, of average height and slim with a skinny moustache and thinning on top with short hair. He is a lawyer and does work for people on welfare who cannot afford much. That comes from wishing that he had someone to go to when he struggled with losing his friend 37 years ago. He also has two kids who are the same age as Jack's. His father is a teacher, and his mother is a secretary.

William and Jack have stayed in contact and even have their kids play together.

DANIEL DISAPPEARED on Wednesday 27th October 1982. A number of things happened on that night that now seem strange.

Around five o'clock, Daniel went round to Bill's parents' house to ask if he would come with him. Bill could see how important it was to him. But Bill did not want to miss his favourite television programme called "Batfink". Daniel explained that he thought he had found something really interesting. He was carrying his 'Instant Camera' and black notebook. He told Bill that he had the story of the century; that he would single-handedly bring down something he did not quite understand. Bill was puzzled as he glanced alternately at the television, his front door and Daniel. It was the new second series of the show, and he was torn between seeing it and going out on a potentially boring excursion. He pursed his lips as he made a tough decision. After a few seconds, he opted for the cartoon.

Daniel sulked as he slowly walked down the steps to go it alone.

AFTER SEVEN O'CLOCK, he was on edge and kept thinking that someone was watching him. His clothes were slightly grubby from where he had been earlier that afternoon.

He noticed two people in a car, parked in a bay facing the police station, across the road. They seemed to have nothing to do and were drinking beer.

He ignored them, went into the police station and walked up to the counter. He wanted to report what he had witnessed earlier and also to explain that he had evidence kept in a safe place. The police clerk behind the counter asked what wanted. Daniel wanted to speak to a detective about what he thought had been a crime. He was not quite sure whether it was a misdemeanour or serious. The police officer found him amusing and told him that he would find someone from the back.

Daniel took a seat on a side bench in the lobby while he waited for a detective. Something was worrying him, and he felt unsafe. He quickly left the police station and started to head home.

The police clerk was the last to see him.

THE SAME NIGHT, the police were rushed off their feet attending various incidents. It was a night that was still being talked about years later, especially as it happened on the same night as Daniel's disappearance. Any other night, the police would be twiddling their thumbs with nothing major to deal with.

The local newspaper company, 'The McDowell News', recorded the stories that night as well.

THE FIRST INCIDENT had been a truck on fire. It would appear that someone stole the truck for a joy ride before driving deep into the woods and setting it on fire. The sheriff accused hoodlums of coming into town from elsewhere and causing trouble by stealing cars. The sheriff could not prove who the offender or offenders were. The police had to call the fire department as the person who phoned it in, who refused to give a name, had not called them.

The second incident involved a resident complaining of some things missing from his garage. He reported a hacksaw and some chemicals missing. The man could not understand why someone would steal them. He had more valuable goods that he would have expected the person to steal.

A final incident involved a car being stolen from a residential home and it ended up being dumped near the woods. The car had no damage, nothing had been stolen from it and the keys had been left in the car. The police contacted the owner to say that they had found it. No one had been arrested.

THE SEARCH for Daniel initially lasted for two weeks, and, by the third, began to lose momentum. There were many posters around the town with a picture of him to jog memories. The searches included the forest on the edge of the Blue Ridge Mountains.

By the fourth week, the cap had been found in the accommodation of a casual labourer. An explanation of why he had it was not given.

Within a couple of weeks, the court had convicted the labourer of the disappearance. They presumed he had killed the boy and gave him life with no parole.

DANIEL'S PARENTS spent months and years trying to get the man to tell them where their boy was. Each time, the man kept saying that he did not harm him. He never gave his alibi for his whereabouts to avoid going to prison.

YOU NEED TO GET OUT

Present Day.

MY NAME IS STOANE COLD, and I have been retired for three years. I have a wife and two grown-up children who are at college. They are about to return for their second and fourth year of college after their summer holiday.

I am black with a round fresh face as black does not crack. I have white thin afro hair cut at grade one. I clip my own hair to save having to go to the barbers. I am six foot and four inches tall with some pudginess due to age. I am fifty-five years old, and, in my heyday, I used to be much slimmer.

I have a dry sense of humour and some people do not know how to take me. When I am working and I sense someone interfering with the case, I can be blunt with them and call out the elephant in the room. It riles people on high profile cases that are seen as sensitive. I care more about the families affected by the crime.

I have written a couple of non-fiction books relating to my experience as a detective and how to find the right clues to solve a crime efficiently. They have done rather well and have brought me a steady income, so I do not have to leave the house to work.

MY WIFE's name is Sheila. Sheila is also black and fifty-four years of age with a slim frame; she stands at five foot six inches. Her thick hair is grey, still with some black strands, and she ties it up in a bun at the back. Her face is oval-shaped with high cheek bones and filled-out cheeks. Her skin is the same texture as mine, dark brown and flawless. Her hands are dainty with fairly long fingers like piano players' hands.

Her mind is methodical which you have to be in her occupation. She is placid and does not let life stress her out. She likes the house to be clean and tidied regularly and feels that I am under her feet all the time.

She works as a Forensic Pathologist and gained a doctorate through her previous employer. She worked for the medical examiner's office in New Jersey for thirty years. When my wife decided to bite the bullet and go it alone, she did not know if she had made the right choice. However, her reputation preceded her, and she was inundated with work.

We met when we were on a particular case, and I had to liaise with her. We clicked straight away. We are happily married, still with a healthy sex life in our fifties.

OUR CHILDREN ARE both boys and of similar build. Their names are Josh and William, and they are studying law and science respectively.

Josh is lanky at six foot two, with a round head like mine and a baby face.

William is similar but he has an oblong baby face.

They both dress in T-Shirts, baggy single-tone shirts and dark blue jeans. They are happy-go-lucky with no worries in the world.

IT HAS JUST GONE seven in the morning, and we are in the kitchen having our coffee. Sheila leaves for work at half-past eight for a nine o'clock start. I have a job interview at a D.I.Y store as she keeps moaning at me for being grumpy, bored and hassling her about when she will be home. My interview is at ten o'clock.

I pour out another cup of black coffee while I think about my interview. 'I told you, it is at ten o'clock.'

Sheila tuts at me, 'You need to get out of the house, right? You do know that. All you do is moan about what the neighbour did today, spying on people coming and going in the neighbourhood.'

I roll my eyes while I have my back to her. 'I can't help it if I can't get the detective bug out of me. Besides, I know Mrs Englewood has buried her husband under the patio. He has been gone for a while now. I just have to go over there when she is not there; just for five minutes. Check for loose dirt.'

Sheila nags at me again; 'You are not going round there to accuse her of killing her husband. She is ninety years old. She hasn't even got the strength to lift a dead weight.'

My three decades of being a cop convince me, 'She got her dead-beat son to do it.'

. . .

SHEILA SHAKES her head at me. 'Well, when you find the body, I will do an autopsy. You need to get out. Oh, and what do I see out of the kitchen window? Mr Englewood coming out to pick the paper up. He may look dead, but he is not.'

I show annoyance; 'Might be someone dressed as him.'

My wife walks over and puts her arm around me and finds me funny; 'You definitely need to get a job.'

We end up kissing and I feel frisky. I check my watch for the time and suggest we quickly go upstairs. She groans about needing to go to work and eventually gives in. She suggests we get adventurous and do it on the kitchen work top.

I like the sound of that, and I help her on the counter. I pull down my trousers and pull her pants down. After all these years, I find her as sexy as the day we met. I cannot imagine being with anyone else.

I have no patience as I'm flustered getting myself inside her. We are so hot for each other that we are rampant and there is no etiquette.

As I thrust in and out, our two sons walk in, and they are mortified. We did not expect them to be coming home so soon. They went away for a camping trip with friends. We quickly adjust ourselves and I struggle to pull my trousers up. We feel like we are teenagers and our parents have caught us.

Our children show disgust, cover their eyes and tell us off as if they are the adults.

Josh says, 'Why don't you use your room? I have to use that counter to butter my toast. Where else have you done it, so I know not to sit there or make my breakfast?'

Sheila snaps, 'Hey, respect your parents. We pay the bills here, so we can do it wherever we want. If you don't like it, move out.'

Sheila and I finish up preparing to go, she to work and me to an interview.

I ARRIVE at the Home Depot in Orange Street about twenty minutes ahead of my interview. I decide to walk around the depot to get a feel for where I could be working. I pay special attention to the staff wandering around, waiting for members of the public to ask for help. I try to picture myself wearing their cargo trousers with polo shirt and apron. With my detective hat on, I catch sight of a couple of staff members and assess who I will be working with.

I actually do not need this job and I'm only doing it for Sheila's sanity.

NOW MY INTERVIEW IS DUE, and I ask a member of staff where the office is. I then go upstairs to a door that leads to a back office with a couple of chairs outside. There is no window, so you are not able to see inside. There are no personnel walking past.

The door finally opens, and a middle-aged man asks me to come in. He must be twenty years younger than me. I do not think I can have him as a boss when I probably know more than him. This cannot exactly be a difficult job.

I TAKE a seat in front of his desk, and he commences the interview. I assess him and can see he has a bit of weight around his stomach and his black hair is thinning on top. His nails are short and look like they have been bitten. His name, which I learned from the email inviting me for an interview, is Frank Caster.

FRANK LEANS BACK in his chair, staring at my printed CV and occasionally glancing at me. 'Tell me about yourself.'

I am not sure if he means personally or workwise and so, I guess; 'I used to be a cop.'

Frank raises his eyebrows. 'I see here you were a detective. I bet you saw a few horrific murders. Did you let anyone get away?'

I already hate this guy. 'There was one homicide. He sliced someone's throat. No one caught him. He murdered six women. Took a cold case to find how many people he had killed and to catch him.'

Frank's jaw drops. 'So, you worked in homicide. What was the worst case you worked on?'

I decide to scare him, so I give the details; 'Well, several years ago, there was an axe murderer. He actually lived round here. We arrested him. But he recently escaped prison. I believe he came to this actual store to buy his tools. We had a suspicion that he worked here. While interviewing him, he kept on saying that he had an axe to grind with a store manager. He never told us his name. It was he who had sent him on his path of destruction. How long have you been here?'

FRANK, overcome with fear, says, 'He...worked here? How long ago did you say?'

I begin to read his mind; 'You been here long? I'm sure it was before you started here. He told us he worked here between 1990 and 1995. You weren't here then, were you?'

Frank's brow is beginning to sweat, 'Huh um. Did you say 1995?'

I had read about my interviewer, and it mentioned he started in 1994. 'Yeah. But I could have got it wrong, and he left in 1994.'

Frank quickly wants to move on, so he continues, 'Well, I'm sure that was another store manager. I have good relations with all my staff.'

I try not to smirk. 'Is there anything else you would like to know?'

Frank almost loses his momentum. 'Right. How did you hear about this position?'

I heard about the vacancy online but said, 'I come here often. I see that everyone working here is happy. So, I thought I would ask a member of staff. All they had were good things to say.'

Frank's facial expression lights up; 'So, why do you want to work at this company? Oh, you already answered that. Why do you want this job?'

I remind him, 'The person I asked about this job made it sound exciting.'

Frank loses his place in the thought process, 'Of course. Why should we hire you?'

I think on my feet for an answer even though I will not have sleepless nights if I do not get this job. 'I can read people. Know what they want if they are struggling.'

Frank perks up and is interested to know; 'Give me an example.'

'If you don't mind, I will use you as an example.'

Frank is confident that I will not be able to read him. 'I see your nails are bitten. That tells me that you are either bored in your job or giving up a habit.'

Frank is open-mouthed, 'How did you deduce that?'

I throw my arms in the air and shrug; 'Well, I have that gift. I would say the job. Maybe things are not going well. Based on your job, performance. Your boss is breathing down your neck. You're not a smoker as I do not see an ashtray on your desk or smell smoke.'

Frank comes over quite shocked; 'What else can you tell me?'

I check for any photos. 'I guess you are either single or separated. I do not see a picture of family or a partner on your desk. So, either you privately don't like your family, or you've never been married.'

Frank cannot believe how good I am. 'Wow. Let's move on. Where do you see yourself in five years' time?'

I avoid the bit about doing his job, 'I expect to work up to customer care. Dealing with customer returns or complaints.'

Frank does not show any expression. 'Okay. What's your ideal company?'

I think back to what I sensed when walking in here; 'Good feel of being in a family.'

Frank likes my answer, and he smiles before asking, 'Why should I hire you?'

I make this up from whatever pops into my head. 'As I said before, I can read people. Work out what they really want and guide them. Easy to approach...'

. . .

SUDDENLY, I can hear a faint police siren gradually getting louder. It distracts me from my answer to the question. There is a window behind Frank and so I peer out to see if I can work out where the police cars are going.

Frank even turns round in his chair to glance out of the window to see what the commotion is.

There are four of them rolling into the car park. The noise of the sirens instantly stops. I stand up and walk over to the window next to Frank. We glance at each other and then at the car park.

Both of us are interested in what is going on and both go downstairs and outside.

ONCE THERE, I am keen for Frank to ask what is going on so I can find out myself. I watch him as I wait impatiently to find out who they have come to see.

A police officer climbs out of the leading car. 'I have come to find Stoane Cold. I am told he is going for some job interview. Can you get the store manager?'

Frank has a puzzled look as he says, 'I am the store manager.'

The police officer in his dark blue uniform waits impatiently, 'Well, have you seen Stoane Cold? He is meant to be being interviewed by you.'

I walk to the side of Frank and answer, 'That would be me. I assume that this is not a social call.'

The police officer has a deadpan expression; 'Can you come with us, please? I have been ordered to come get you.'

I turn to Frank with a curious expression and ask, 'Have I got the job?'

Frank is speechless and does not answer.

A small crowd is now forming behind us and fanning around. I have an idea that I will not fill the position.

WILL YOU?

While travelling in one of the four police cars, second from the front, I wonder where they are taking me. While I am sat in the back, separated by a clear plastic partition, I try to observe any key landmarks to determine where in Washington they are taking me, but nothing seems to stand out.

I turn round in the back seat to see if the two police cars behind us still have their lights flashing and they have. I feel like a celebrity with my own carriage.

Eventually, we arrive in a leafy suburb of Washington. I think we are a few miles away from Capitol Hill. We travel through an area with white picket-fenced homes on either side with grassy sidewalks. As we continue along the street, the landscape eventually changes to wealthy homes. It feels strange that these mansions are in the same street, just a few hundred yards along.

I feel the car slowing down abruptly and then we take a sharp turn into a narrow drive that is a shallow horseshoe-shaped entrance. The residence is a brilliant white townhouse with ivy sparsely covering the front and with vines showing through the leaves.

The front of the house is symmetrical with four columns of Victorian high windows. I wonder who could be living here.

THE POLICE OFFICER tells me to wait until he steps out of the car and opens my door. He tells me that the owner is expecting me and apologises for the theatrics. I give a half-smile and ignore his sincerity and walk alone to the front door.

I push the doorbell, then, a few moments later, a tall slim butler, clean-shaven with thinning grey hair, answers. I expect him to ask me to introduce myself, but he was already waiting for me. He tells me to walk along the wide hallway and turn left at the end.

There is a wide white marble staircase to my right, like a slip road, and it narrows as you follow the railing up the stairs. There are two extravagant ornaments on either side of the stairs; life-size white porcelain statues of humans in compromising positions. You would think you could see up their legs and expect their stone feminine parts to show.

When I reach the wall at the end, I follow the butler's directions and see an open entrance.

WHEN I GO INSIDE, I notice there are people in the room already, all in plain clothes. All four men acknowledge me straightaway and greet me with smiles. I curiously smile and wait for one of them to explain.

THE MEN ARE of similar build and appearance, aged between their thirties and late forties. One of them is fidgety, clutching a slim pile of papers. He looks to be the youngest and ready to leave. Another man seems to be giving him a final spiel about a written speech. The third man is sat with his briefcase open and putting things away in it. The fourth man seems to be leading them.

A woman comes in; she is wearing a brown short skirt suit and appears to be in her late twenties. I cannot work out if she is a secretary or a personal assistant here to support him. She walks briskly around the room looking for something before leaving again without anything.

I remain standing, waiting for someone to greet me, while I observe them going about their working lives. Five minutes later, everyone leaves the room and that only leaves a conservative Caucasian man with short dark hair speckled with grey.

HE HAS a full oblong face with a pale complexion, so pale he looks like he has never seen the sun. He allows himself to relax and collect himself, before putting his hand out towards me. I hesitantly shake his hand not knowing who he is or what his background is.

Just as I am thinking I could do with a black coffee; the butler walks in, and the man gives him the order. The butler looks down his nose at me as he floats out of the room. I shake my head at him and smirk, not believing how he carries himself.

THE MAN INTRODUCES HIMSELF. 'Hi. Hope that I did not make you uneasy. I spoke to your wife asking where you were, then sent police cars to pick you up. There is a matter of urgency. So, I couldn't wait to see you at your home. Sorry; your face looks blank. I am Senator Charleston, Frank Charleston. I'm waffling now. How did you get your name? Appropriate for what I am about to ask you.'

I have not had the chance to get a word in edgeways to ask why I am here. 'You have a nice house. Must have cost you a few bobs'

Senator Charleston chuckles in response. 'I didn't used to be a senator. I was originally a farmer from an old town called Marion. Heard of it?'

I slowly shake my head before replying, 'No. So why am I here? I should be helping customers find their tulips.'

Senator Charleston half laughs as he loses his momentum, 'There is a favour that I need. I was told you are the best. I want something solved that has been left lying for twenty years.'

His butler interrupts and passes me my coffee in an elegant teacup which I did not expect. I look at his butler with a disappointed expression and take a sip. I tell him to go on.

Senator Charleston thinks back to what he was saying, then continues, 'Yes. I am about to be re-elected. I have a few months before election to keep a promise. Among other things, it is what got me elected in the first place. I thought once I reached Capitol Hill, I would leave that town behind me.'

He is not making sense to me, and I want to speed this along to get home, so I ask, 'What exactly did you promise and what has that got to do with finding a detective?'

Senator Charleston is getting agitated and goes for a walk around the room. 'A kid went missing back in 1982. It was never solved. A man went to prison for it, but there was no substantial evidence found apart from a cap belonging to the child. No witnesses came forward.'

I am confused now. 'If there was no body found, how did you convict someone of it? How did you find the man who supposedly made the kid disappear? Finally, how did you prove he did it with no evidence or witness?'

Senator Charleston has guilt on his face and sits back down, 'Back then, things were different. A black man came into town for a few months. When the kid went missing, they automatically assumed it was him. Nothing happens in Marion and so, when a kid goes missing, it is a big deal and happened to coincide with the wandering black man. They could not prove or disprove it was him who took the kid. There has not been an incident before or since.'

I wonder what backward town would get away with an arrest like that. 'So, if you somehow proved he did it, why re-open the case? You know you can only make new enquiries if there is anything worth looking into. Just because you say he is innocent, that is not going to set him free.'

Senator Charleston goes quiet and cannot make eye contact. 'The prisoner has claimed his innocence for years...'

I have had enough of the tiptoeing about, so I persist; 'Yeah. That is what usually happens. What are you not telling me, Senator? I have a gorgeous wife to get back to and kids to prevent from eating us out of house and home.'

Senator Charleston leans closer to me and confided, 'I just know he is innocent. I went to see him. I have a knack for telling if a person is lying. It is a gift. I have had it all my life. Spend a few days down there. Feel it out. If you think there is nothing, then I will accept that.'

I know he is not telling me everything and wonder if he...a woman comes into the room without a care in the world. She calls the senator 'honey' and I assume it is his wife. His posture and mood change as he smiles at her and introduces her to me as Janice. She is in her own little world, oblivious to my reason for being here. She asks her husband who I am and gives me a stare which asks, 'Why is there a black man in our house?'

I finish my beverage. 'Well, I think I will get going. Thanks for the coffee.'

Janice continues to stare at me as she wraps her arms around Frank. 'So, are you going to take the case? An innocent black man is in prison and is going to face the death penalty in a few weeks. It may be pushed forward. There is an old president leaving, if you hadn't noticed, and he doesn't like black people. He is signing executions off left, right and centre.'

Now that is what Frank failed to mention! 'You want me to find the missing body, take samples from the body and prove or disprove that he did it. Thirty-eight years is a long time to whine that you are innocent.'

Janice has hope in her eyes; 'So, you will take the case?'

Before I do, I need two answers - 'Why did you pick me? There are a hundred good detectives still on the force. And how did you find me?'

Senator Charleston's throat goes in as he swallows. 'I made some enquiries. All said that you are the best. I had your cell phone tracked.'

I think the contrary; 'I am only seen as the best because I am thorough. Don't leave anything unturned. It is being overworked, prioritising easy cases, laziness and problems at home that make a bad detective. Being good at your job has nothing to do with how many cases you solve. It is attention to detail.'

I see Janice smiling with delight, 'Why are you in agreement with your husband?'

Janice is adamant that her husband is right. 'If he says someone is inno-cent, then they are innocent. He can see it in people's eyes.'

I eventually pander to him, 'Okay. I will review the case, look at the evidence and see this guy in prison. If I have any ounce that he is guilty, I walk.'

Senator Charleston is happy with that and says, 'That is all I am asking you to do. But I am confident that you will find a discrepancy to prove he is innocent. I forgot to mention the money. I will be hiring you as a private eye. Whether you believe him or not, I want to find the boy's body. I made a promise to the family when I had my campaign to be elected. I plan on still honouring the promises I made during election time. How does twenty thousand dollars plus expenses seem? Just spend a few days. If you don't catch a whiff, I will accept that.'

I think about my book sales and my wife's income; 'I am rich enough. I don't need your money. But I will take the case. You have piqued my interest. When is his date of execution?'

Frank and Janice go quiet, and Frank eventually answers, 'In two weeks' time.'

Now, they are taking the biscuit. 'Two weeks? To find a body, fresh evidence, new witnesses, examine the cap with the latest technology in forensic. Two weeks is going to be a stretch.'

Senator Charleston has one more thing to say; 'I have to warn you. Things have not changed. It is a forgotten town that never moved with the times. It may be in California, but they are still cliquey with minority people.'

I roll my eyes. 'Maybe I will take the twenty thousand.'

Janice interrupts, 'They are nice people. But their mindset is still stuck in the sixties. You will face racial tension, but under the surface. You being the only one who can solve the case, it will cause friction.'

Great; more problems; 'I'll live. Where's this prison?'

Senator Charleston has something else to say - 'Aren't you going to ask me what his name is?'

I do not create a familiarity with the dead victim as it clouds my work, so I explain, 'I didn't ask on purpose.'

Senator Charleston still tells me; 'Daniel Harris. He was six years old.'

I ignore his last comment and ask, 'Who is the man in prison?'

Senator Charleston appears candid when he tells me, 'Jefferson. Alex Jefferson. He worked on my farm, and you get to know people really quick. I have a sense for people.'

There is nothing else to discuss so I leave to go home and pack.

4

RETURN TO INNOCENCE

I arrive home a little after five o'clock after being driven home in one of the four cop cars, that stayed behind. Before I left the senator's house, he told me that the accused is at Alameda County Santa Rita Jail.

I GO into the kitchen to pour out a glass of red wine from the bottle already opened on the counter next to the side of the oven. I then take it to the living room and sit down in the armchair and mull over about still visiting the man in prison. I wonder what I will achieve by seeing him.

As I consider the fact that I can read people's faces, I hear someone open the front door and eventually walk into the living room. It is my wife, Sheila.

Sheila gives me a curious look; 'How did your job interview go? I assume you got it.'

I am still in deep thought as I answer, 'You won't believe what happened today.'

Sheila looks annoyed as she is standing in front of me, 'How hard is it to get a job in a hardware store? What did you do, analyse him and tell him how shit he is at his job?'

I smile at her comment; 'Better. I went there for a job and ended up getting a case worth twenty grand.'

I sip on my glass of red wine, 'We don't need twenty grand.'

Sheila is still standing in front of me. 'That is what I told him. So, I'm doing it for free.'

Sheila is getting snappy now; 'What does it involve?'

I make myself feel more comfortable in the armchair by having my arms opened out. 'That is the thing. It means going back to what I said I would never do, but it gets me out from under your feet. However, it does mean going away for a few days.'

Sheila slumps on the sofa and gets in a sulk. 'Where?'

I take another sip and take my time savouring the flavour as I stare at the glass; 'Marion.'

Sheila exhales loudly and asks, 'Where the hell is that?'

I unenthusiastically tell her, 'North Carolina.'

Sheila rolls her eyes. 'The look on your face tells me that it will be a few days.'

I take the last gulp before replying, 'Try a week; two weeks maximum.'

Sheila looks deflated, 'What's the case?'

I gather my thoughts as my head is fussy now; 'A missing child. Presumed dead but no leads.'

Sheila is sympathetic but wonders, 'So why you? You're retired.'

I feel personally bored and wanted something challenging. Working in a hardware store would have sent me to an early grave.

I pretend to be disappointed. 'My name came up a few times. They think only I can solve the case. I felt obliged to say yes.'

Sheila knows me after all these years. 'You couldn't say no. When do you leave?'

I hesitate, not knowing if she will get mad at me, before admitting, 'Tomorrow.'

Sheila does not show any emotion. 'You better make sure you find out what happened to that kid.'

I think the same, considering I am travelling across America. 'There is one other thing.'

Nothing is going to surprise her now; 'What, Stoane?'

I wish I had not brought it up. 'They have a convicted man in jail waiting for the electric chair.'

Sheila sits up and I can see she knows I have to do this. 'So, do we get a chance to sit down for breakfast?'

I am thinking that we will not have any time alone for a while, so I suggest, 'Why don't we have some time together? The kids will not interrupt us.'

SHEILA LIKES THE IDEA, and we go upstairs to have some time together. I chase her up the stairs and after all these years, I find her bum very sexy as I follow it. We do not make it to the bedroom as we collapse on the landing floor and embrace in a kiss. We fight to get our suit trousers off and then take our pants off.

She surprises me that she is not wearing her granny pants today and causes me to slow down. She was not wearing these briefs this morning when we had sex on the kitchen counter.

SHE HAS on her sexy red lacy briefs that accentuate her curves. As I take my time taking her pants off, I inhale her fragrance which arouses me. Sheila smiles at me knowing how I get turned on by her body. I read her mind and begin to caress her vagina.

She still likes to be clean-shaven which I cannot understand. In my days, hair was all the rage. The hairier the better. But social media and magazines have encouraged my wife to be completely shaven. I do not particularly have a preference as I love her just the same.

It is only now that both our kids are at college, that we have time together again to play catch up on the sex we have been missing out on.

Sheila, as usual, murmurs as I stimulate her clitoris, feeling her becoming aroused. Her thighs are now slightly trembling as she is about to have an orgasm. Her feet point straight while her body tenses and I hear her groaning quietly. She catches her breath to tell me that she wants me inside her.

We decide to have sex in the bedroom so as not to mess the carpet on the landing.

WE ONLY MAKE it to the edge of the bed as I enter inside her from behind. She raises her bum in the air as she knows I like the view of her pert bum. I am ready to burst as I enter inside her and feel the tightness of her damp vagina. I enjoy seeing my shaft sliding in and out and watching my cock form a glistening film along my length, created by her.

Sheila rests her knees on the bed and lies flat on her thighs with her feet resting over the edge of the bed. This allows her to receive me deeper inside her. Us older generation also know a trick or two.

It is not long before I feel myself beginning to cum; that sets her off again and we both cum at the same time, groaning loudly. Once I cannot take the ecstasy anymore, I collapse on her back and we both laugh; we have missed this.

Sheila pants heavily, 'God...I missed...that.'

I do not think she has missed it as much as I have; 'I...love...giving you... one from...behind. You still have a great body after more than thirty years of marriage and having two babies.'

Sheila hums in agreement, 'Well, working long days without food and being on my feet does it.'

We both get on the bed properly and hug each other as we lie on top of the bedsheets. We discuss my trip away and she suggests travelling down if it becomes more than two weeks. I ask if she can keep me company throughout the time over there, but she has work commitments.

After we have recovered and finish talking, we decide to have another session but in the traditional position.

TUESDAY DAY 1

IT IS the next morning and we are all sat at the family table having breakfast together. We are all dressed and ready to leave right after breakfast. The four of us are quiet with nothing to say. Our kids already know that I will be away for a couple of weeks as we told them before breakfast.

Josh asks me about my trip. 'Why do you have to go to wherever you are going, again?'

He makes me smile, 'They have an unsolved case.'

Josh wants more detail, 'Loads of people disappear. What is so special about this case of a disappearance?'

I know he has a valid point. 'Well, someone promised a family, after being elected, that he would put their loss to rest. He made that promise in his first term. He is now coming to the end of his second term and going for his third.'

Josh has confusion on his face. 'So, why didn't he follow through with his promise in the first term?'

Sheila interrupts, 'Exactly. That is politicians for you.'

I ignore my wife's comment. 'Well, it has taken a death sentence to do something about it. He believes the man is innocent.'

Josh is still confused; 'I thought white people didn't like black people.'

I chuckle at his comment. 'Not all white people hate black people. Also, we need to raise our heads above that because we answer to God, not white people. If we stoop to their level, we end up going to hell like them, the ones who are racist. Not all white people are racist. You can blame the media for that.'

Sheila adds to that, 'Listen to your father. I work with some great colleagues who are not all black or any other ethnic group. We stay true to ourselves and change the world with respect and kindness, not becoming like them.'

I USE this trip as an example; 'I will be heading into a hostile environment. The town has had only one kid go missing. They blamed the one and only black man in the village. They have animosity against black people. They will be pissed when they see a black man solving the case. Instead of retaliating like them and by solving the case and keeping my head high, I will prove to them that black people are not like they view us.'

Sheila smiles at my teaching and rubs the back of Josh's head as she walks behind him to clear the table. William is happy just listening to the conversation without voicing his opinion.

AFTER WE HAVE FINISHED BREAKFAST, I hug my kids individually and tell them that I will miss them. Being young adults, they grunt, and I just about hear them telling me to stay safe. It is now only my wife and I left in the house.

Sheila quickly loads the dishwasher before heading to work. I rest my elbows on the aisle counter as I lean forward to stare at my wife bending over. Sheila catches me and finds it amusing.

She stops partway through loading the dishes and stands up straight. 'How are you getting there when you only met the man yesterday?'

All that had already been arranged before leaving the senator's house, so I can tell her, 'Having someone pick me up and travelling by private jet. With a hire car waiting for me at the other end.'

Sheila is starting to see the ramifications of this case. 'This is not a matter of saving face and shutting up the family that he promised years ago. This is close to his heart.'

I nod my head in agreement. 'I asked a few questions, and you know how I read people.'

Sheila shakes her head. 'You know that.'

I look down to gather my thoughts then say, 'I asked him why he believes the man is innocent.'

Sheila is impatient; 'And?'

I think back to how Senator Charleston reacted; 'When he told me that he thinks he is innocent, his eyes looked up and to the left.'

Sheila has some understanding of my meaning; 'Yes, that is when someone is recalling a memory. If you look up and right, you are imagining.'

I have a theory. 'I think he knows why he is innocent but does not want to put himself in the crossfire to affect his election. I didn't push him. I just listened. He also put his hand on his forehead and looked down a couple of times.'

Sheila racks her brain for what that means; 'Isn't that when you have something to be embarrassed about?'

I tell her she is close; 'It is when someone feels ashamed of something. But he is willing to take a risk of solving the case despite his past potentially coming out. The guilt is catching up with him.'

Sheila has that look that she always gives me when she has a gut feeling that the wrong person has been arrested. 'You know what I am going to tell you.'

I know that look. 'I am going to see the man facing the death sentence. If he shows me the tell-tale signs, I will find the real killer.'

Sheila looks sad as she says, 'You assume the boy was killed?'

I know the patterns of a murder, so I answer, 'The body would have been found already if it had been an accident. The person would have found a way of having the body surface. A murderer who did it out of passion would not have hidden the body. Made it disappear. A calculating murderer would make sure the body was never found. Look at the drug cartel. They go to great lengths to hide a murdered body unless they want to make a statement.'

Sheila nods in agreement as she listens to me.

EVENTUALLY, it is time for her to go to work and we embrace, knowing that we will not be seeing each other for a while. In fact, it might be some months.

When she leaves, I go into the living room and wait for my ride. It will be here by twelve midday.

5

YOUR SIDE OF THE STORY

A local taxi comes to pick me up and sounds the car horn to get my attention. I know that I do not need to check my luggage. I already have my single medium-sized suitcase with two weeks' worth of clothes with the anticipation of only being there for that length of time.

As I walk towards the taxi along the path from our house, the driver meets me a quarter of the way and takes my suitcase. I get in the back of the car while he places it in the trunk.

The driver confirms my destination, which is Newark Airport, a twenty-minute drive away. He is not talkative and so I sit in silence during the journey there.

When we reach the airport, he drives to the private hangars which is a separate route inside the premises.

Senator Charleston is lending me his private jet to fly directly to the nearest airport to Marion, which is Rutherford County Airport, then it is a thirty-minute drive to Marion Correctional Institution. I will have a rental car ready for me to drive to the jail and then Marion. That is an eleven-minute drive to the town. So, everything is amenable.

My stay will be in a trailer park at Lake James Forest RV Park. I chose this as my home for my time there.

It feels strange avoiding the security checks and walking onto a plane straight from a taxi.

A steward takes my suitcase from the taxi driver and places it into the storage compartment under the plane while I climb aboard.

After ten minutes of preparing for flight, we are waiting for permission to taxi along the runway. It is close to one o'clock when we leave.

I am told that it will take two hours to land outside Marion.

During the flight, I rest my eyes as I have no report on the case to peruse or any information on the town. I will literally be going in cold.

The pilot asks for my name, so he knows what name to address me by. When I initially tell him, he is speechless and does not know if I am trying to be humorous. I get this all the time and am so used to people's reactions when they hear my name for the first time.

Just like with everyone else, I explain how my parents chose my name after I was born. Apparently, after I came into the world, I gave a stone-cold face of being upset from being dragged out of my mother. I never showed happiness in the first six months of being born. So, my parents thought it would be amusing to give my first name as Stoane Cold. Since being a cop, I have continued to have a hard look on my face. My wife thought I hated her when we first met, and it was not until began to get to know me that she realised it is just the way I come across.

Her parents trusted her that she was making the right choice in marrying me.

The pilot decides to call me 'Mr Cold' to avoid any awkwardness for him when getting my attention. I understand and tell him that I am used to it and whatever makes him relaxed is fine by me.

I manage to sleep for an hour and a half before I naturally wake up and see the time on my watch as gone two-thirty. I should be landing before three o'clock. I plan on still seeing this gentleman in prison tonight before I head to my accommodation. It will be a further forty minutes of driving from the Airport to prison and then Marion, so it will be close to seven o'clock tonight before I get there. That will be plenty of time to unwind, speak to Sheila and then have an early night ready for my first day solving the disappearance of the kid.

I have a late lunch of a prawn sandwich and two biscuits to go with black coffee before we land in half an hour. It feels strange being served food on a private plane. I thought the interior would be superior, but it looks like it is straight out of the sixties. The plane seems very basic with no mod cons like USB portals, electric chairs or a decent screen for watching a movie. The senator must have got a bargain when he bought this.

I look out the window with bleary eyes to see the sun starting to go low in the distance. There are clouds casting a dark shadow over the sun but no signs of rain.

I WAS RIGHT; we land around three o'clock and allow for ten minutes to find a hangar to park up and then let me out. The pilot calls me Mr Cold again when he says goodbye and hopes that I enjoyed the flight. I tell him it was good, and the food was nice.

I thought the rental car would arrive here but thinking about it, the car hire people would not know which hangar to leave it in.

I wait to see where the steward and pilot will go to see if I can tag along to get to the airport building, then find the car rental shop. As I process my thoughts, a couple of cars arrive. One of those cars, the grey Ford saloon, is mine, so, I can go from here to the prison.

APART FROM A COUPLE OF TURNS, it is a straight run and takes thirty minutes to get there, arriving just ten minutes before five o'clock.

When I arrive at the gate, the security guard does not have me scheduled to come in. He phones the prison while I wait in the car for a response. He is one of those typical guards with black aviation sunglasses. It must be part of their standard uniform. Eventually, he lets me through the gate.

I assume that because I had no time of arrival, the senator must have told them that I would be here at some point, hence my name not being on their list of visitors.

I can't remember the last time I visited a prison to interview an acquaintance of the person I was bringing to justice. That familiar smell. Why do prisons always smell the same? Also, they all look the same to me.

This prison allows visitors to see inmates in a disused canteen hall, which will make our conversation more relaxed. No prying ears listening in on our conversation.

Before they bring out the prisoner, I am taken to the hall first. I still do not know his name as I never asked the senator, and I will find out now. The room can house about two hundred prisoners, so I assume they have more than one canteen to allow everyone to eat at the same time. The room is a little chilly as it is no longer used and so the heating is not on.

I am left waiting for ten minutes. All I can think about is finding a restaurant to have dinner. My stomach is craving food.

Finally, they bring him in with two prison guards accompanying him with chains around his ankles. He has a confused expression which tells me he has not been told of my arrival. I can guess that either the senator never met him, or he was too busy to update him. I will get to that bit later.

THE MAN IS TALL, close to my height and bald. He is in his fifties, although he looks much younger, with typical smooth black skin.

He has a full, round face, and his body is slim but solid with slim arms and his hands are big with long fingers. I imagine whether his hands could harm a child or if his stature could be strong enough to carry one away.

He does not resemble a typical prisoner with a chip on his shoulder, who moans, 'Life dealt me a bad hand.' He comes across as placid and with nothing to hide as he stares at me with curiosity. There is no hostility in his eyes towards me; it's as if he has been disturbed from watching his favourite television show.

He appears to be healthy considering that prison does not like convicts who harm children.

I LOOK at the two guards and ask for the chains around the prisoner's ankles and wrists to be taken off as there is nowhere, he can escape to. I do not feel threatened by him, and they know that he would not try anything that might remove his privileges for good behaviour. I wait for the guards to wait outside as they close the door with a clang.

I motion him to sit at the nearest table to us on a metal bench. I sit opposite him and break the ice.

While I study his posture and his hands clasped together, I ask how he is. 'Has your stay been comfortable over the last twenty years?'

He shows confusion and asks, 'Why are you asking me that? Who are you? I was not expecting you.'

I notice he keeps his eyes fixed on me with an honest response. 'When is the last time you had anyone come and visit you?'

He shrugs his shoulders and moves his head to his right. 'I don't know. I don't exactly have any family.'

After only a couple of questions, I can already read his body language. 'What is your name?'

He shrugs his shoulders again and looks down to the right again. 'You should know. You have come to see me.'

I want to ask the important questions now that I have a baseline to go by. 'Your name, please. I was sent here.'

He exhales then says, 'Jefferson. Alex Jefferson.'

I introduce myself before he asks, 'My name is Stoane Cold.'

Alex lets out a chuckle, 'You are kidding. Seriously?'

As I said before, I always get this reaction. 'Yes. I can leave.'

Alex suddenly stops laughing, 'That's cold. Literally. Your parents must have hated you.'

I move the conversation along. 'Yeah. Now, I have been asked to review a cold case. I've been asked to prove your innocence.'

Alex's eyes light up with surprise as he says, 'So, why now, twenty years later?'

I mention the electric chair. 'When your life is going to end, it kind of raises eyebrows.'

Alex's face tells me that he is ready to leave this earth. 'It takes an appointment with death to suddenly listen to what I have said all along. My story has never varied,' he tells me while staring straight at me.

'Let me hear it,' I insist.

Alex is vexed now and frustrated as I think the past is all coming back to him. 'Aren't you going to be writing something down?'

I get short with him; 'I have a good memory. Besides, I will be looking at all the transcript and interviews. So, I only need to listen.'

Alex's eyes raise up to the left as he thinks back thirty-eight years ago. 'I was seeing someone at the time. I'm not proud of it as they were married. What made it worst was that the person was white. Things were different back then. I was passing through town not expecting to hang around that long. I worked in the fields. I ended up falling for the wrong person. If I gave their name up, no one would believe me. They will think I am out of my mind. They will definitely think I did it as I will be seen as a wacko.'

I am curious about why he is not giving up the person's name now as he is facing death row, so I push for information. 'You're going to die now. Times have changed. What was the name of the woman you were seeing? Let me get her to say for the record.'

Alex is getting frustrated as he looks up at the ceiling. 'I can't. It will ruin her career.'

I cannot believe what I am hearing. 'So, your life is less important than hers. You do know you are going to die. If you were with this person, what did the police link you to? They must have had some kind of evidence.'

Alex gets angry, then tells me, 'They found a baseball cap in my accommodation. It was not there before I left.'

I interrupt him, 'Where was it found?'

Alex is still pent up as he explains, 'I asked them. After finally going to trial, they told the judge they found it on the floor in the living room. The first time I saw that cap was in court. I had never seen it before in my life.'

I kind of believe him but keep an open mind. 'When did you leave your place and when did you come back?'

Alex is really thinking now. 'Now you're asking me. It is over thirty years ago. I think it was around six-thirty when I left, then came back about eleven. I went straight to bed.'

I wonder why he did not see the cap when he came in, so I probe a bit more; 'When you walked into your place, where did you walk in?'

'When you walked in, you either went into the living room or towards the bedroom. So, I would not have seen the cap unless I chose to watch TV before going to bed. If I had seen the cap there with blood on it, I would have panicked and wonder what to do with it. I would not have walked past it and thought nothing of it.'

I can see the pain behind his eyes and understand his frustration, so to reassure him, I continue, 'I will find the body and use it to find the killer.

Forensics has come a long way since 1982. I promise you that I will find out who your alibi is. That is my job.'

Alex let out a loud breath as if that would happen; 'Good luck with that. Not in a million years will they come forward and back up where I was.'

All I need to be told is I can't, and I am like a red rag to a bull. 'If I find you are innocent, I <u>will</u> find them and I will get them done for perjury. I promise you that.'

Alex is speechless and sees that I am not just saying these words. I slam the table to indicate to the guards that I am finished here. He has really riled me up and I don't want to slap him so hard his head spins. The guards put his chains back on and Alex turns his head and stares at me as he is taken back to his cell. I now have my motivation to tear this case apart.

6

BACK IN TIME

As I drive towards Marion, I need to top up with gas as I did not realise that the tank was low. These hire cars are meant to be filled up for the next driver.

The only road that takes you into and out of Marion is a clean black tarmac with fresh road markings. Leaves are strewn along the side of the road and there is thick woodland on either side. There is no one else on the road tonight.

The fuel light comes on which worries me. I don't relish being stranded in the middle of nowhere. I hope I can reach a gas station sooner rather than later. Even though it is only another ten-minute drive, it does not feel I am near any civilisation. There are no houses around to stop and ask for assistance.

While I consider my options, I catch a glimpse of a faint light up ahead on my left and hope it is a house. I can then ask for help to find a gas station. It does not take long to approach the light and realise that it is, in fact, a gas station. I am relieved and now I hope it is actually open as it was a streetlight I saw from the distance.

WHEN I STOP NEXT to one of the pumps, I look through the car door window to see if the pump is open. The pump is one of those sixties' styles and so it's hard to work out if I can use it.

I get out of the car and notice the shop has dim lighting and I walk over to peer in the window to see if it is open or if it is night-time lights.

Suddenly, I am spooked when I hear an old croaky male voice. I picture the person being in his seventies wearing dungarees with a lumberjack shirt and an old cowboy hat. When I turn towards where the voice is coming from, my guess is not far off.

THE MAN HAS a beard that is turning grey and scraggly. He is Caucasian, slightly bent and very slim like he has not had food for weeks. He asks if I need assistance.

I give him a friendly smile, so he does not feel threatened by a black guy, remembering what Senator Charleston told me about Marion. But the man is totally oblivious of whether he should be afraid of me or thinks I'm a non-threat.

He walks over to my car and fills up for me while I stand next to him. I decide to ask him if he is aware of the disappearance of the child.

I make pleasant conversation first. 'Do you get many people travelling along this road at night? I haven't seen one car.'

The old man scratches his beard. 'I guess you are coming here to find out who took that boy?'

I do not know how to respond. 'You live out here? Or do you live in town?'

The old man continues about the missing boy; 'Rumour has it that a black man is coming into town to solve the murder. We don't have black folks here.'

I find him interesting, so I try to get some more information. 'Why do you think he was murdered?'

The old man stares into the pitch-black before answering, 'He's never been found.'

I play devil's advocate; 'Could have gone somewhere and had an accident.'

The old man turns to me with a glare. 'Nah. That poor child was murdered. You find that man who did it. Don't leave until you do.'

For some reason, I lower my voice; 'That's what I plan on doing. Will I face hostility?'

The old man shows no concern in his voice, 'Only from some hillbillies who none of the townspeople get on with. So don't take offense if they try to give you hassle. I don't think they like black people.'

I am curious as to whether I will face friction; 'Will the people be co-operative?'

The old man does not have conviction in his voice when he says, 'I think so?'

I am intrigued to know what he was doing on the day when the boy was reported as missing. 'Where were you back then?'

The old man murmurs to himself. 'Stuck here. I don't live in town. I live right here. Only see people like you come and go. Visitors. I hear a lot when people stop here for snacks and gas.'

I want to know about the child's parents, 'Are the parents of the child still around, had more children or moved because the memories are too much?'

The old man turns to me again. 'Oh yeah. They never had anywhere to go. No family outside of town.'

I wonder if they have knowledge of the case reopening, even rumours flying around. 'Are they expecting me to go and see them?'

The old man takes his time with an answer; 'They will assume that you will go to their house for an interview or clues from his bedroom. They have left that room from the day he never came home.'

The old man finished fuelling my car five minutes ago and I get out cash to pay him, assuming there is not card machine here. I realise that I never asked his name and tells me it is John. I tell him my name, and, for the first time, he never quizzes it. It is like nothing fazes him in life.

He tells me to have a safe journey and will see me when I leave after solving the case.

I EVENTUALLY REACH the town and look for a restaurant that is still open. I stop outside the first place I see. They do not have their food places close together. I am really hungry now.

It is a BBQ place called 'Smokey Que's' and so I will be getting a chicken meal.

THE RESTAURANT IS DATED as I would expect, with a painted wooden interior in black, white and brown. They have today's dishes written in chalk. A few people look over when they see me. I know that they will know I am from out of town based on this being a tight-knit community. They do not look at me like I have two heads, but they definitely know I am not local. I wait at their lectern, that is the shape of a lecture stand, to be seated. It is quiet considering it is a school night.

A young Caucasian waitress with brunette hair and dull red lipstick greets me and walks me over to a window table. She asks how my day was and I tell her it was quiet.

I assess the people here and quickly learn that these people live a simple life and do not look for trouble. I assume they keep to themselves and can imagine they only had one missing child and were totally shocked that it happened. Alex was a drifter and so they thought it had to be him. They could not possibly have a resident involved. I can imagine that the sheriff and the police station will be similar to here.

I notice the standard glance that only ethnic groups would understand. I remember my wife always saying that there are two types of people; The 'Overt' kind and the 'Covert' kind. These are the 'Covert' kind. They think they are not racist, but they accidentally become racist.

The best way to describe it is like going to the zoo. Everyone will relate to this, even the ethnic group of which I am one. Imagine that there is an odd-looking animal that is not appealing to the eyes. A person who is not racist will see beyond its appearance and see that it is a nice animal. A racist person will either vocalise their opinion, saying the animal is ugly, or will pull a face but not say anything. The person who vocalises will be 'Overt' and the person who pulls a face and does not say anything is 'Covert'.

The people in the restaurant are 'Covert' as they stare without realising that they are being racist. It is not just a glance at a new face. The waitress who greeted me is the person who notices I am new in town. But she is young and is still learning, while those of the older generation have passed the learning stage.

I can understand why ethnic groups gravitate to cosmopolitan cities where their existence is not unheard of.

IT DOES NOT TAKE LONG before my order comes out; steak and chips with salad... It looks really good and tastes just as good. When the waitress comes over to ask if the food is okay, I ask her if she has grown up here. I pick up that she has a southern accent, which I did not register when she took my order. She confirms to me that she has lived here all her life and I ask her what it is like to live round here. She tells me that nothing happens here, and crime is next to nothing. Her response resonates with me in regard to what it must have been like, never to have an answer to what happened to one of their own. It must have felt like an alien abduction, constantly wondering where they had been taken.

She asks where I have travelled from as she knows I am not local. I smile at her good observation and say that I am passing through. She has a curious look and is not embarrassed to say that they do not have many black people or other ethnic people visiting. I appreciate her honesty and ask if there will be any trouble. She smiles at me and says that there is never any trouble with folks passing through. She also mentions my appearance saying that with my looks, I won't have any trouble at all. I wonder if she was coming on to me considering she must be the same age as my kids. I half-smile not knowing how to react.

I finally finish my dinner and wait for her to come and take my money. Once I pay, she tells me to make sure I come again while I am in town. I tell her that I will certainly do that and then leave.

I HEAD to the Lake James Forest RV Park for a good night's rest. It is only an eleven-minute drive from the restaurant.

I park up outside the reception and walk in. It is a trailer converted into a reception area. A lady, who looks like she is in her forties, is behind the desk. I tell her that I booked one of her trailers earlier this morning. She looks at me and then asks why I am staying here when there are nice hotels to stay at. I have my own reasons and tell her that I want a cheap place today. I hope that does not insult her.

Her eyes peer down her nose, through her thin reading glasses, sizing me up and then she asks my name. I am too tired to have another conversation about my name and tell her it is Mr Cold. She tries to be funny by asking if my personality is the same. I do not dignify her with an answer as she smiles at me.

She walks me to my trailer and starts explaining the rules. She says I cannot have prostitutes in the trailer and no drugs in the trailer or on site. No loud music or parties after eight o'clock in the evening and then she repeats herself with the 'no prostitutes' rule.

I try not to laugh while I listen to her rules and wonder if she has seen everything in this park. I wonder what the other residents are like here and if I will hear them during the night.

She does not mention her name, so I check her blouse for a name tag. Her badge says her name is Justine Brown.

JUSTINE IS Caucasian and aged forty-seven. Her skin is fair with a slight yellowness and her face is aged from years of smoking cigarettes.

She is a little paunchy standing at five foot six with slim legs and a filled-out stomach. Her hair is light brown and greasy with streaks of grey. She wears it down and it falls just above her shoulder.

She is wearing tight light-blue jean shorts just above her knees with a green plaid shirt hanging out and unbuttoned with a white T-Shirt underneath.

She is brash and seems to be without a care in the world. She can come across as rude unintentionally. If any of the residents that stay here catch her eye, she is not shy in coming forward.

She is single with no kids of her own and does not do anything in her spare time apart from reading a book in the reception trailer. She lives on the site and manages it. She watches everyone that comes and goes very closely.

The moment she saw the new tenant come in, she took a shine and is hoping he will stay a while. She wants to try to get him into bed before he leaves. She eyed his behind while showing him the trailer and paid no attention to his wedding band. She guesses that he has split from his wife and that's why he is now living in a trailer park.

WHEN SHE HAS FINISHED SHOWING me around inside the trailer, she leaves me to settle in. I notice the bed is next to the open kitchen and a small round table with two chairs. The shower room is behind the wall where the bed is. The toilet is the next room behind the shower. The floor has a thin worn blue carpet throughout. You can hear the floor creak occasionally as you walk through. The walls are thin so I can understand why there is no loud noise after eight.

I unpack my suitcase and put my clothes in a built-in slim wardrobe and underwear in a drawer next to the bed.

When I am finished unpacking, I call my wife and let her know that I have arrived here safely. I have not properly checked out my facilities but will do that after I get off the phone.

The phone rings three times before she picks up, 'Hi. I'm here now.'

Sheila is happy to hear from me. 'How was the trip?'

I recall the flight; 'It was strange not having to go through check-in and security.'

Sheila moves on to Alex; 'What was he like?'

I think back to our conversation. 'Not what I expected.'

Sheila wants to know what my thoughts were; 'Do you believe him?'

I have already made my mind up about his alibi. 'Yeah. But his witness is a mistress. He only has his loyalty. He does not want to shame her. But she has not visited him once.'

Sheila asks if there was more; 'Was there anything else?'

I remember Alex not knowing who I was, so tell her, 'The senator never visited him. He had no idea I was going to be there. But the prison did. He lied to me.'

Sheila thinks of a reason why he would have lied. 'He wanted to find a way of getting you there.'

I do not agree with her suggestion. 'There is something not quite right. I will find out. Anyway, I need to get ready for bed. Speak to you later.'

Sheila has nothing more to say, 'Well, thanks for calling. Kids miss you. I have an early start tomorrow.'

I feel tired after my trip now and I want to go to bed. 'Yeah. Speak to you later.'

When I finish talking to my wife, I have a look around to see what there is here.

THERE IS a kettle and sachets of tea, coffee and sugar. The kettle is a travel-size one that can boil enough water for two cups of coffee. I have a double bed with brown bedsheets and brown thick curtains.

I chose to stay here rather than a nice hotel because I want witnesses to feel comfortable enough to approach me. From my own experience, people feel more comfortable in their own environment rather than inside a police station. If I stayed in a five-star hotel, I would not be reachable for people to come forward.

When I was a detective, I had to go to their home or social place to gather crucial information. I never once had a person walk into the station to ask for me.

Once I change the bedsheets for my own and move the pillows away, I go to sleep. I will buy new pillows tomorrow.

I have to ask for a Bob Terrace when I arrive there for ten o'clock and he will give me everything I want including the original report on the investigation at the time. But I also have my kind of investigation; thinking outside the box.

7

ONE SINGLE BOX

Tuesday Day 1

I CANNOT TELL what time it is. I do not rely on an alarm clock and allow myself to wake up naturally. I am my own boss and have a few months before Alex has to be executed. So, I will make my investigations in my own time.

I check my cell phone for the time and see it is after eight o'clock. I need to find a place that does breakfast as I feel sick. I did not factor in that I need to have a café nearby where I can have breakfast each day. I should have checked for accommodation near a café as well as a restaurant.

I search on my phone for a local place to eat which will become my daily place to visit. Once I find a café, I try out the shower, hoping the showerhead is a good sprinkler.

EVERYWHERE IS between five and fifteen minutes' drive away. You can set your watch by it. The nearest place is 'Crook Door Coffee House' which is at the bottom of the road, a seven-minute drive. I am surprised it is modern. It is shaped like a galley kitchen, long and narrow. The flooring is laminated with a wood effect. The front of the cafe has black-framed windows that go all the way across. Inside, the restaurant is L-shaped with the payment desk at the end. The tables run along either side. The clientele are different from the place I went to last night. The customers do not appear to be bothered by seeing a new face walk in. I think I made the right choice.

I order scrambled egg with bacon and sausages. I am conscious of the time as I want to be on time at the Marion Police Department, on Main Street.

I have already mentally listed the things that I need to get started; things that are not standard in a homicide investigation. Living like the locals within the poor community and breathing in the way the victim lived, helps me to get a better understanding of why they were killed.

I have a hunch that always comes out of the blue without me pre-empting it. It is a gut feeling that I never ignore. I get out my cell phone and add my thoughts to my 'Note' app. By the time I finish my breakfast, I have all my thoughts typed down.

WHEN I ARRIVE outside the police department, I notice that the building is made out of red brickwork and has a strip of sandstone wall for the middle section of the building. There are steps made out of white concrete leading up to the entrance.

I notice that there are parking bays opposite the building across the street, facing the department.

I WALK into the lobby of the police department on time and speak to the man behind the desk who is busy with his head down staring at a form.

He is Caucasian, tall and thin with a shaven balding head. He appears to be in his fifties with a faint tan and wearing rectangular silver-rimmed reading glasses. His nose is thin and pointy.

He is aware I am standing in front of him even though he has not looked up. I tell him that Bob Terrace is expecting me. I wait for him to move his head up as he asks who is asking. I tell him my name and that doesn't cause him to look up.

He tells me that he is busy and will take a while. I look behind him at the open-plan main office and then look behind me at the small empty lobby. I turn back to him and show a confused face as there are no persons in the lobby and the staff in the office are not rushing around.

I would hate to see what it was like on a quiet day. Everyone would be walking backwards.

I tell the clerk that I will sit down in one of the empty chairs by the wall.

The penny eventually drops, and he realises that I was being sarcastic as he takes his reading glasses from his face and glares at me.

I smile at him after I sit down to ease the tension. Knowing how quiet it is today, in this day and age, it must have been super-quiet twenty years ago. The whole department must have been looking for that child.

THE CLERK CALLS my name and says that Sheriff Bob Terrace is ready to see me. He opens the counter door to allow me to walk through. Some staff glance at me in turn as I walk past their desks to get to the sheriff's office. They try to be discreet, but I know they are expecting me.

Through the window, I can see him sitting at his desk.

HE CARRIES little weight around his stomach and has thick dark grey hair, combed back. He has a trimmed grey beard as well. He is likely the original sheriff from when the boy disappeared. He stands up and walks from behind his desk to greet me with his hands out.

He is almost my height with thick short fingers and a hard grip as I shake his hand. He motions me to sit down.

I initiate the conversation. 'Senator Charleston asked me to look into the missing child.'

Sheriff Bob corrects me; 'Dead child. I was here when it happened. I had my assistant officer dig out what we had in the archive. What makes you able to solve a forty-year-old case?'

From his negative attitude, I can see he is not interested. 'I've had a knack for solving tough cases. When a case was not going anywhere, muggins had to resolve it. Only because everyone was stretched and could not be asked to follow up on all the leads. Also, they did not want to follow the leads. Rather it comes to them.'

Sheriff Bob does not come across as confident that I will solve the case; 'I think you have made a wasted trip. I have been here ten years and not one person has come forward with new information. Before that, my predecessor never had anything further.'

I am not sure if he is from around here, so I ask, 'Were you brought up around here?'

Sheriff Bob is slouched in his chair like he doesn't want to be here. 'I was here when the boy disappeared. I grew up around here. It was big back then. Nothing like that before or since. It was on all the news. This is a tight-knit community. If anyone knew, they would have spoken out already.'

I understand what he is saying but I have also dealt with local communities. 'People still don't talk. They don't want to rat on their former neighbour, either in case of repercussions or because they are related. People know and don't realise it.'

Sheriff Bob perks up with a puzzled expression at my comment; 'How do people know without realising?'

I explain, 'There was a case a few years back when I was still on the force. A salesman travelled from one state to another. People gave different stories of seeing him about town. But no one saw him get murdered. The witnesses were interviewed across a three-month period, across two states and three cop departments. There was no communication between them. Each had a separate open case reference. He was seeing three different women. They never knew each other. He was married. It was the wife who reported him missing first as she saw him every week. Reported him missing after a week. The other three women reported him a week later. He saw the three women once a week. People going missing are a dime a dozen, so why would he be any different? One night, the wife came in, crying, drunk and at her wit's end with no update after six months. The clerk didn't want anything to do with the woman. She was not making sense. He just wanted to get rid of her and so passed her on to the nearest person he could find. That was me, ready to go home after a long shift writing up a case I solved. My boss wanted it written up that day. Like you, I was fed up after a long day, my wife nagging at me for not being home yet. So, I go to fob her off thinking she was a drunken waste of space. But her clothes; a watch was bugging me. The watch and the clothes. The watch was at least two thousand dollars. That told me that she was not a waste of space.'

Sheriff Bob is getting impatient with the story, 'So what happened?'

I make it brief, 'I went to his employer. Got a pattern of where he travelled. Asked how they kept tabs on him. Followed the places he visited on a map. Then looked for police departments in those areas. Assumed he pissed off a husband, understanding how a salesman works. Then contacted those police departments asking for all missing salesman. There was only three reported. I asked for the files. Different names, of course. Looked at the witnesses' statements then marked them on the map. Witnesses that never met each other drew a trail. Interviewed the three mistresses that reported him missing to build my case. Neither witness ever knew that they had solved the case. I was right. He pissed off a husband. Looked at husbands with a criminal record. Solved a six-month case in a week.'

Sheriff Bob's face drops, 'How the heck did you come up with that?'

I smile at him now that I have his attention, 'I also used local newspapers and morgues along the trail of where he had been. One page story, at the back of the paper and one morgue with a John Doe. You see, no one ever talks in a community.'

Sheriff Bob smiles at me, 'Well, what are we waiting for? I'll get the evidence.'

I watch him open his door and shout across the open-plan office, calling for his assistant named Timothy. He nervously stands up and says 'yep'. Then realises why his name is called out and brings in the box. He almost drops it, being nervous after having his name yelled out. He passes it over to Sheriff Bob and babbles 'boss' to him.

Timothy notices me and gives me a quick smile.

TIMOTHY IS slim and almost six feet tall. He is younger than the sheriff and I can guess he is in his sixties. His full head of hair is black and brushed back with gel. He comes across as bumbling and not confident. But I sense it is a front by the way his eyes shift around the room. It is like he is trying to find out what is going on.

He would have been around in 1982 as well.

WHEN SHERIFF BOB gets a single box and puts it on his desk, I take the lid off and peer inside. I can see that I need room to take everything out and lay it in some kind of order. Then I wonder where to begin my investigation. I want to work through the evidence methodically.

I lift the box to see how heavy it is to get an indication of how much evidence there is to go through. As I anticipate the weight, the box almost comes shooting out of my hands.

8

INSIDE THE BOX

I can see the sheriff is not too thrilled at me using his office as a dump to go through the evidence. So, I take the hint and find an empty desk somewhere in the main office to use.

One of the detectives sees what I am trying to do and points me in the direction of a small room that I can use for privacy.

AFTER I GO INSIDE, I see a table that is big enough to lay all the contents out. I head back outside to ask a random person for a pen and paper. Another detective, who is on the phone, digs out a notepad from his desk drawer and a pen in a stationery container. I gesture my appreciation and go back inside to review the evidence. I want to follow a flow to help speed up the process of finding Daniel.

I take each item out one at a time. They are as follows:

Foolscap folder

Inside are a few pages of manuscript relating to people's written statements. I flick through the pages to see the names of the eyewitnesses. I begin writing notes as reminders of things I need to make new enquiries about. I want to interview witnesses myself to hear them in their own words. Written statements can be improvised and conformed. I like to hear the witness talk on the fly where they do not think about how they describe the scene or the story.

I want to interview them, and their names are James, Marty and Nancy. Their statement says that they were sat in a car opposite the police station.

They are also apparently the last to see the boy walk round the corner of the police station. I want to see if they have more to say.

I also notice that there are what appears to be the missing boys' friends giving their input. Their names are William, Bill and Jack. I assume they were giving a character witness and details of the last time they saw him. I also want to interview them, and I'm hoping they still live here.

I also remember what the senator and Jefferson told me about the cap being found in his place of temporary residence. So, I try to see if the folder has any report on that finding. I want to speak to the person who found the cap.

BASEBALL CAP

I see the item in a plastic bag, and I press the film against the cap so I can see if there is any soil on it. I notice that there is a bloodstain inside the rim where it rests on the forehead. There are also some loose specks of what seems like bark or brown leaf. I cannot really differentiate between the two.

The cap is made out of denim material, but the blue colour is worn. There is no logo on it.

I assume that back in 1982 they did not have DNA testing and there has been no reason to test it as it has been confirmed by the boy's parents.

I want to use the blood on the cap to compare to the body, when I find it, as proof of Daniel, assuming it is his blood.

PHOTOS

There are only pictures of the boy's bedroom and I have no idea why. The crime did not take place there and no evidence in the box was taken from his bedroom. There are a few pictures and I study them to see what is in his bedroom.

I can see detective books for kids and normal school stationery on his study desk. One thing that brings to mind is that there is no diary. Using my lateral thinking, if the boy had an interest in investigating, it would make sense to have a notepad, a notebook or diary to record his findings. There are no items of that description on his desk. He must have had that on him at the time of his abduction or I am overthinking.

Videotape

This is the last item in the box which is, as you would expect, a VHS tape. VHS was short for Video Home System. I don't think the police station will have a tape player. I will have to have this transferred to a digital format. Either on a USB, compact disk or a digital versatile disc which is commonly known as DVD. I am praying that this town has a store that deals with old technology and can convert them.

I wonder what is on the video for it to be in evidence...

I FINISH MAKING my notes on the four individual items. I rearrange my notes on a new page, prioritising which evidence to go over first and last.

After about five minutes, I make my final list of what order to investigate. This will be as follows:

WITNESSES

James, Marty and Nancy - I will recheck what they saw and see if there are any discrepancies.

William, Bill and Jack - find out what Daniel liked and where they hung out as friends.

Video

I will get the tape converted and see what is on it and see if there is anything I can question further.

BASEBALL CAP

I will get the DNA when I find the boy's body. I do not want to waste time focusing on this when there are others that I can deal with now.

I DO NOT FIND the photos of his bedroom to be of any relevance. Now I have put the three other items in order of investigation, I feel the need to find out what the newspapers reported. I have a niggly feeling that more than a disappearance happened in October 1982. It is a gut feeling I have rather than any information I have discovered.

I put everything back in the box and plan on holding onto it by taking it back to my trailer. One of the things I like about cold cases - no one misses the evidence and there is no deadline to meet. Also, no expectations of solving the case.

When I am finished putting everything back in the box, I let the sheriff know and then ask if he knows of the witnesses.

.   .   .

BOB TELLS me that he is aware of the three men in the car and that they hang out at a rough bar. They have had some interaction with the law but generally, they keep themselves below the radar.

I explain that I will be going to interview them first at some point. I mention that the last pieces of intelligence will be any newspaper reports on the case as well as any coverage from the time of the disappearance.

Bob tells me that it would have been covered by a newspaper called 'The McDowell News' at 136 N Logan Street. I thank him and as I go to head for the newspaper office, he asks if I am hungry. He wants to go for lunch and asks me to join him. I check my watch and realise that it is close to one o'clock.

He knows a place where we can go for lunch. I oblige and let him take the lead.

We get into his police car, and he drives us to Jim's Country Style Restaurant on Main Street which is a minute's drive from the station.

THE RESTAURANT MAKES TRADITIONAL STEAK, burgers and fries as well as salads, however, we just order sandwiches instead with coffee. I have my usual black coffee made to my liking. I have a particular strength that I like, and they make it just right.

While tucking into our food, I have some queries answered. 'How does it feel to be reminded every day that you did not find the body? How long did his parents come to the station?'

Bob shows no expression and groans, 'It took a while to accept that we would never find the body. It took two years before they stopped coming to the station every month. It was hard to see their faces with no good news to tell them.'

I understand where he is coming from. 'I get that. What with your other commitments and a man in jail for it? You got something.'

Bob still does not feel any better. 'I used to go and see him every couple of months to find out if he would tell me what he did with the boy. Each time, I felt this would be the time he told me. But he gave the same answer every time. I stopped asking after three years.'

I change the subject and ask about the boy. 'What do remember about Daniel?'

Bob takes a while to remember, then says, 'He was a run-of-the-mill kid. Nothing out of the ordinary.'

I think about the video and ask, 'What is on the tape I saw in the box?'

Bob remembers straight away. 'Witnesses said that they saw Daniel coming out of the police station.'

I remember this from briefly reading the statement on the guys in the car. 'Yeah, I read that they saw him walking around the corner. I didn't read the part where they saw him walking out of the police station.'

Bob recollects the three men giving the statement; 'Yeah. The tape was a part of the prosecutor's case.'

I think out loud about the baseball cap being found. 'Someone found the cap in Alex's accommodation, on the farm. Did you question why someone knew that an item of Daniel's clothing was there?'

Bob has a quizzical expression; 'Things happened so fast back then; I did not get a chance to question that. By the time they jailed him, it was an afterthought.'

I ask him the question to spark a debate; 'So, there is a boy that goes missing. After a few hours, the parents report him missing. Everyone is focused on finding the child, right?'

Bob is curious to know where the conversation is going. 'Yeah?'

'Everyone is instructed to search nearby places. At what point would you have an idea about going round someone's house with no tip-off? And magically find a boy's cap lying in plain sight? Why would you kidnap a boy, discard the boy, come home and then go back out again? He was not even in the search. A killer will help out in a search to check if anyone finds the body. There was no clothing of his covered in blood or linked to the boy. Don't you find that odd?'

Bob is beginning to follow where I am coming from. 'I can't explain it. Now you have mentioned it, I am guessing Alex is innocent after all. Hence why he won't tell us where the body is.'

I continue; 'From my years of experience, a killer will make sure the body cannot be found. They would also not leave any evidence of being involved in the crime. If they kept a souvenir, it would be well hidden, not left on the side for anyone to find. Alex has no previous criminal activity. He had no connection to the boy. He was never witnessed stalking kids or seen wandering the town. The farm owner believed in his innocence. A black man of all things.'

Bob is thinking even more of his innocence. 'He never changed his story once. He never gave up his witness.'

I have already been thinking about that, so I tell him, 'I will find who is his supporting alibi. And crucify him for allowing an innocent man going to jail.'

Bob has a question; 'Do you think you will find the body? It's been thirty-eight years. We couldn't and there were close to a hundred of us.'

I have a technique, 'There is something I have in mind. It will mean looking beyond the evidence. Build a bigger picture. Also, forensics has come a long way in the last thirty-eight years. If there is a strand that gives us a clue, I will find it.'

We finish our lunch, and he drives us back to the police station. I use my cell phone for directions to the newspaper office.

9

READ IT IN THE PAPER

The newspaper office is on the same road as Jim's Country Style Restaurant but a few hundred yards down.

After I park up, I see that the business has a shop window, so you can see staff working inside. When I walk into reception, I see a bell on the counter. I wait for someone to notice me first, but they seem to be keeping to themselves, staring at their computer screens. I leave it a couple of minutes before tapping the bell.

A young woman in her thirties with a young face walks over to greet me with a welcoming smile. She wouldn't have been born when Daniel Harris went missing. He would be 44 years old today and possibly married with kids.

When she comes over, she is friendly and asks, 'How can I help?'

I find her friendliness infectious. 'Are you always this welcoming?'

She takes a pen and paper from the counter and gushes, 'You are not from around here.'

I find her intriguing. 'Very astute for a journalist. I'm passing through. Looking into something. Could you provide an article going as far back as 1982? I am reaching out on a limb.'

She does not show surprise and says, 'Yep. A particular period?'

I almost forget what I have come for, then remember the date. 'The...27th October.'

She is interested in my enquiry; ''Why that particular day?'

I wonder if she knows the story. 'Someone went missing. I have been asked to look into it. Nothing exciting.'

Her eyes light up. 'You wouldn't be looking into a boy called Daniel, would you? Everyone knows the story about a missing boy. Parents ended up threatening us that we would go missing if we misbehaved like Daniel.'

I half chortle at the idea of there being a legend. 'I guess your parents told you about the story?'

She gets enthusiastic and continues, 'I should know, my father used to work here, and he was the main reporter on the case. He spent weeks investigating the disappearance. It almost became an obsession at the time. He was convinced that he would solve the mystery before he retired.'

I do not want the conversation to end, so I probe deeper; 'What happened in the end? To your father.'

She reflects back as her eyes gaze past me. 'It almost drove him to despair. He felt that he could help the police by persuading people to come forward with any information. It was the biggest thing in this town back then, apparently.'

Eventually, she asks who I am; 'What is your name and what do you do for a living?'

I wonder what her reaction will be to my name; 'You will only laugh. Everyone does.'

She is intrigued now; 'I promise I won't laugh. If I do, I will give you everything on what we have on the boy.'

I am not sure if she is flirting with me and if she knows I am wearing a ring. 'Stoane Cold. I'm a detective. Retired.'

She tries to be funny; 'As in sober?'

I've never heard that one before; 'Something like that.'

She introduces herself; 'My name is Jessica McDowell.'

I realise the significance of her surname and say, 'I guess that your family own the newspaper.'

Jessica smiles awkwardly. 'Something like that. Now you know that I help run the business, I'll let you inside and you can help yourself.'

I FOLLOW BEHIND her as we walk through the small open-plan office towards the back. There are about fifteen staff in the office, all with their heads down getting on with their work. No one glances up to see who is walking past with Jessica.

She questions my accent; 'Where are you from? New York?'

I find her sociable and reply, 'New Jersey. But everyone assumes that we are all New Yorkers.'

JESSICA EVENTUALLY TAKES me to a microfiche machine. It appears to be modern with a desktop flat-screen monitor and an oblong box next to it.

I get shown how to use it briefly and she makes a point of making sure I come to her if I have any problems.

· · ·

I HAVE some grey field boxes to choose the day, month and year and can also enter a keyword to find a specific article. I want to do two searches - any reports of that night and any articles about the boy. I enter the date first to find out what other incidents took place on 28th October 1982, reported in the next day's paper.

After I press 'Enter', a few seconds later only three events come up. These are a truck on fire, a robbery and a stolen car.

There were no other major stories reported from that night. Any other news was related to the town's normal day-to-day running and traditions.

I find a way of printing the three articles for myself to help build up a picture of what happened that night.

My brain helps to solve a puzzle by seeing everything that makes up the story, no matter if it is menial, like the house being robbed. I like to build up a storyboard as if I am the screenwriter of a television show. That way, I do not miss anything vital.

When I get back to the trailer, I will put the three articles and items from the box up on the wall. I will create a crazy wall linking certain items together, such as the cap and where it was found in Alex's accommodation.

JESSICA COMES over to see how I am getting on as I wait for the copies to come out of the printer. I forget that I am not in a police station and wonder if she will be upset at me for using her company's assets.

I wait for her to say something about me helping myself to private property.

Jessica approaches me with a smile, 'You got everything you wanted? Hope you worked out the printer okay. Is there anything else you need?'

I am pleasantly surprised to find her okay with helping myself. 'There is nothing else I need. I really appreciate your help.'

Jessica is hesitant as I prepare to leave; 'Where are you staying?'

I mention the trailer park. 'It helps me to get a feel of a town by living amongst the people. A hotel makes it feel like a vacation and putting a proverbial time limit on my stay.'

Jessica shows pity on her face as she asks, 'Do you have decent food in the trailer?'

I go blank thinking what decent food is, so I tell her, 'I was going to go back to the same restaurant I went to when I got here.'

Jessica frowns at my answer. 'Where is that?'

I try to recollect the place. 'It was Smokey Que's.'

Jessica sighs, 'You're coming home to my parents. They will give you a square meal.'

I feel a bit overwhelmed by her welcome and say, 'You don't have to do that.'

Jessica is forward. 'I insist. We can take these things back to your trailer and then come over. I will tell my parents to pull up another chair. We normally eat at seven o'clock. My mum has an hour and a half to rustle something up.'

I can see she will not take no for an answer, so I agree; 'Okay. As long as you tell them.'

Jessica calls them as we leave the office.

I LEAVE my car in front of the newspaper office and go in hers. Her driving is slow and smooth. It feels like it will take forever to get to my trailer.

While driving, I ask more about her. 'Did you always want to be a journalist?'

'I would spend hours as a child watching my dad work in the office. I found his work fascinating and wanted one day to do what he did. I was intrigued by the work, not knowing what the job was called or what you need to do the job.'

I can picture her as a child sitting on the floor playing with a toy while watching her dad sat at a desk, finalising tomorrow's front page.

Jessica wants to know about me; 'What made you want to become a cop?'

I still do not know what made me want to join the police force, so I try to explain. 'I wanted to do something else when I was a child. I finished university and felt that I wanted to solve puzzles for a living somehow. I found I had a knack for unravelling difficult crimes; finding an answer to how a person ended up in a certain position with no disturbance in the room. I ended up finding a job that paid me to solve unexplained cases.'

Jessica is hypnotised by my conversation and fascinated that I may have a good chance of solving the disappearance of the boy. She feels the urge to ask if she can tag along as an observer and write about the journey to eventually finding out the truth of what happened to Daniel. I think about how nice it would be to have a person with the knowledge of the area and also to have company. I change the subject to her parents.

'What does your dad do at the office?'

Jessica is quick to explain that he is retired. 'He keeps Mum company. He hasn't worked for about five years now.'

A thought comes to mind about him working on the story of Daniel. 'Did your father get obsessed with Daniel's disappearance? Did he get close to the parents?'

Jessica has a glint in her eyes. 'It almost ruined Mum and Dad's relationship. He spent hours away from home following up one false lead after another. He felt like it could have been me who had gone missing. He could relate to the Harrises and felt compelled to help them find their missing boy. But every possibility was quickly shut down. No one in town had a clue or saw anything. It felt like he had disappeared from the face of the earth.'

I tell her my thoughts; 'When you cannot work out what happened, your mind assumes that something unimaginative happened to help you understand. You think that he up and left town to find closure. You think that he is somewhere living a new life with a new name and no recollection of the past. It is a way to allow your brain to deal with a loss.'

Jessica seems to get where I am coming from. 'Do you think you will find him?'

I tell her how I approach each case; 'I have no target set for myself and my method for solving a mystery has not failed me yet. I put my feelings and personal thoughts aside. I stand outside looking in.'

WHEN WE ARRIVE at the trailer park, she parks outside the front of my accommodation. Jessica stays in the car while I go inside and put the printouts inside my trailer. I quickly place them on my bed and will worry about starting my crazy wall either late tonight or tomorrow morning.

Once I am happy it is tidy inside, I quickly go back out and get back in Jessica's car.

10

A NEW HELPER

When we arrive, I notice the house is a traditional white wooden house and sizeable, considering he owns a newspaper business in town.

I have to walk up some wooden steps to the porch that goes around the front of the house and follows round the side. They have a traditional swinging chair and table with chairs along the porch.

JESSICA USES her house key to let us in and I follow behind her. I wonder what her parents will be like and how they will appear.

I also wonder if they know that their visitor will be a black man, considering I have not seen another black face in this town so far.

As I have these thoughts, her parents come bursting into the reception area to greet their daughter and see who she has brought with her.

Her parents are completely friendly, greeting me with smiles and enthusiasm as her father goes to shake my hand and her mum asks us to come through.

WE GO STRAIGHT into their dining room and the oval dining table is full of choices from roast chicken to roast vegetables and condiments to go with the meal.

Her parents are very welcoming and ask how my first day in town has been. I answer honestly, finding the town very different to New Jersey. I mention that I have not seen a black face in town yet, nor any other ethnic group; not that I have an issue with that, but still the same, everyone is hospitable and friendly.

. . .

THE FAMILY IS Caucasian and have lived in Marion all of their lives.

Jessica has a pale complexion with long light-brown curly hair that falls below her shoulder. Her face is fair with a slim nose and filled out cheeks. She is five feet seven with a slim figure and she is in her thirties.

Her work clothes are slim grey trousers, plain pastel-coloured blouses and tailored tank tops. She is rarely in social clothes.

She studied journalism at university before working at the same newspaper that her dad worked at before he retired.

Her personality is sombre, and she prefers not to be in the limelight. She does not like confrontation and prefers to be a wallflower and observe the world. Even though she knows the answer ninety percent of the time, she would rather hear the answer from the professional person. She would never make someone feel stupid if she knows that person is wrong. She likes to know the truth no matter how much it will hurt.

She became a journalist because she loved how her dad never let go of a news story until the facts came out. She is intrigued by mysterious events and finds them fascinating, like going on a treasure hunt. Her excitement for finding unsolved stories fascinates her and she is yet to come across a solved mystery. She hungers to watch an enigma unfold and eventually get solved.

In her personal life, there is no one special to call a boyfriend but she hungers for a love life. Everyone knows each other in Marion and so it is very hard to find someone you don't know. She has taken a shine to Stoane since he came to her office. She has noticed he is married, from the ring on his left hand, but she still has a fondness for him.

HER DAD IS CALLED Anthony and he is about six feet tall with a thin frame and a full head of light grey hair. He is in his seventies. His face has aged gracefully, that is pale with some redness and clean-shaven. He wears a grey and white faded striped bow tie with a white shirt and faded blue two-piece suit.

He is mild-mannered and enjoys the quiet life. He spends his retirement in the garden, pottering about. He also enjoys reading biographies of interesting people. Also, in his spare time, his mind wanders on old reports he wrote of cases that were left open. One of them is Daniel's and there's not a day that goes by, but he wonders what happened to him. He hoped that he would be found before he retired.

He has kept a scrapbook of his work on the story and keeps it in his home office.

. . .

JESSICA'S MUM'S name is Patricia. She is in her seventies and has been a housewife. She has long thick light brown and grey hair. She has aged well with little wrinkles on her face. Her height is five feet five and she has filled out over the years.

She wears a long ankle-length frilly patterned skirt with a top and cardigan.

Her personality is sociable, and she enjoys having people over for dinner and drinks. She enjoys having after-dinner discussions on current affairs.

She also spends her time keeping the house tidy and reading books.

I FEEL WELCOMED with open arms, not expecting to see such a spread of home-cooked roast dinner. I wonder if they made this especially for me or if this is normal proportions for the three of them.

I notice her mum is happy to see me as she encourages me to feel at home and help myself.

Jessica is asked to sit next to me, and her parents sit at either end of the table.

I sense that Jessica is awkward around me and I'm not sure why. I watch her being observant and studying her parents helping themselves to the glass tray of vegetables. As I learn about her quirky personality, I think that if I had a daughter, I would like her to be like Jessica. I would want my daughter to be inquisitive and question everything. Of course, I love my sons, but they don't care about knowing the truth.

During dinner, we talk about what New Jersey is like and make comparisons with how I perceived Marion. I am honest and say that it was challenging to adjust quickly to the way of life here. I explain that it is a slow pace here and getting information is not looked on as a matter of urgency.

As I talk about this, Tony and Patricia laugh at my description and understand where I am coming from. It is a breath of fresh air having a family acknowledge their culture from the outside. I feel like I can express myself freely without offending or coming across as opinionated. I even mention the annoying parts of living in New Jersey like having no filter.

Jessica continues to observe rather than join in the conversation.

There is no mention of work which is also refreshing. They touch briefly on my black background and ask what it was like growing up. I am honest and say that I mixed with some troubled kids in Harlem. That they did not catch a break. I tell them I did not want to be a detective growing up. My dream was to be an actor and star in the movies, but my interests attracted me to forensics. It was a new thing mixing science with crime.

. . .

THE CONVERSATION MOVES on to my family. 'I have two grown-up children who are at college. My wife, Sheila, is a Forensic Pathologist. She looks at dead bodies all day. Works out what happened to them.'

Jessica is fascinated. 'So, if we found Daniel's body, she would be able to know what happened to him?'

I never thought of that. 'Yes, that's right. But I'm sure you have one here.'

Tony mentions something about that; 'We don't have a pathologist here. So, if you do find the body, we won't be able to find out how he died.'

That does not surprise me. 'I can have my wife come here and do the analysis on the body.'

Patricia is more interested in my kids; 'What are your children's names?'

I really like this family showing an interest in my life, so I tell her, 'Josh and William.'

'What university have they gone to and what are they studying?'

I have to think for a second, then remember, 'Both have gone to New York University to study Law and Science. One wants to do what their mum is doing and the other wants to be a lawyer.'

Patricia continues to show an interest. 'Have you dealt with any other cases similar to this?'

I rack my brain over the last twenty odd years. 'There was one. I came off a day shift when I was finishing off a report on a case that I closed the day before. It was around six o'clock. My wife wanted to check to see what time I would be expected home. Just as I switched off my computer, a woman comes in, nervous and not sure if she is in the right place. I ask if she is looking for someone. She tells me that her daughter has not been home for a couple of days. It was not strange that she would be gone for a couple of days as she was often crashing at friends' places. But this one time, she did not text or call to say where she was. I am thinking of home and seeing my family, but I can't just leave her distraught and alone in the office. So, I call my wife explaining what has happened and take down notes. Missing persons was not my forte, so I passed it on to the relevant department that deals with missing persons. I do not think any more of it. Six months later, a lady comes in and I kind of recognise her, but I don't know where from. Suddenly, I realise that she is the same woman I saw about her missing daughter. I had no idea why she came back. At first, I thought it was to say thanks. However, it turned out that her daughter was never found, and she asked me to take over the case. Before I stepped on anyone's toes, I spoke to the detectives running the case. They had reached a dead end. So, I thought I would look into it. The short version of the story is that I lived in her shoes and walked the last moments of when she was last seen. There was a particular route along a dirt track with trees on either side, acting as a barrier to a sheer cliff drop on either side. I took the time to look for loose footing along the path. When I almost slipped, I then used that spot to safely climb down and see if I could see a body or a piece of fabric matching her clothing. I found her body and called the local police.'

Patricia is keen to find out the outcome; 'What happened to her?'

I say it as it is. 'It happened to be a complete accident. She was taking her normal route, but this time, she misjudged her step. There was no sign of foul play. The forensic pathologist saw no sign of involvement.'

Patricia is fascinated by the story and asks, 'Is that why you are here now, because of your skills?'

I tell her how I ended up coming here. 'A senator wants to finally put the mystery of the missing boy to bed. He went to find the best in the field of cold cases. He claims that the only name that came up repeatedly was mine. He then had police locate me and bring me to his house. I didn't know why I was asked to go with the police officers. I was at a job interview.'

Tony chortles at my story then says, 'You're kidding! You were having a job interview?'

'My wife was fed up with me lazing about at home. So, she made me find a job. I applied to work for a DIY store. Then the cop cars came blazing.'

All three laugh at my story and cannot believe how funny my life is.

WHEN DINNER IS OVER, Patricia and Jessica clear away the plates and serving trays. Tony sips his third glass of red wine and finally turns the conversation to the missing boy.

Anthony is interested in what I have done so far. 'Are you closer to finding out what happened to the boy?'

I let him know what little I have done; 'I have the evidence box that the police station kept in storage. I also gathered articles on the case to pick up a feel for what took place that night. Tomorrow, I begin to go through it all and find the original witnesses and test the original evidence with the latest forensic methods.'

Anthony is interested in my thought process; 'What do you hope to find with the fresh tests?'

'I will look for traces of the suspect and find clues to where they held the boy in the town.'

The women finish clearing away the table and eventually bring in dessert which is homemade apple pie and ice cream. Tony offers more wine, but I remember I have to get Jessica to drop me off to pick my car up.

The conversation changes to Tony telling me about his career and the newspaper being in his family. He is the third generation to own the company.

I ask him how he reported the missing boy. He tells me how Jessica described it in the car, but his version misses out the effect it had on him.

It is not long before I feel it is time for me to leave. I am anxious about starting my crazy wall tonight before I go to bed. I also want to phone my wife before it is too late in the evening.

When I am ready to leave, Jessica makes a point of telling her parents that she needs to take me to my car.

When we are parked up next to my hire car, we stay in her car for a while. I sense she wants to say something to me but I'm not sure what.

She hesitates before saying, 'Can I tag along with you? I mean, to watch your progress and report on it.'

I feel flattered that she wants to observe my work, so I agree. 'Yes. You can follow how the case is progressing. It will mean coming round to my place in the morning at eight o'clock every day, going through the previous day's findings, building up a timeline.'

Jessica has relief on her face. 'I am so grateful. Well, I will see you tomorrow.'

11

LATERAL THINKING

When I get back to the trailer, I notice that it is after ten o'clock. I mentally work out what time I want to go to bed and how much organisation I can achieve with my collection.

Before I begin, I check the kitchen cupboards for a glass and then open my bottle of rum to pour a drink. I take a sip before going over to the printouts I made, which I left on the bed.

I read the words on the papers and begin to build up a number of scenarios in my head, wondering if these can fit into the timeline of Daniel's last steps.

As I let my mind wander, I call my wife to check in and let her know how my day has been. I quickly check the time again as my phone rings. Sheila should still be up as it has not gone eleven yet. I am surprised she has not tried to call me first, but she knows how I do not like to be disturbed when working.

I hear her answer her phone, 'Hi. What are you up to?'

Sheila sounds distracted, 'How was your day?'

'I went to the police station to dig out original evidence. I then went to a newspaper to see if there were any major incidents on the same night. And I ended up being invited round to dinner with the owner of the newspaper company.'

Sheila is interested in knowing more, 'What were they like?'

I briefly describe them, 'It is a family of three. Their daughter now runs the company and appears hands-on. You wouldn't think she manages the place. It was her who invited me. They were hospitable and made sure I had enough to eat. Now, the daughter wants to tag along and report the investigation.'

Sheila chortles. 'How old is she?'

I know she is slightly jealous, so I say, 'Jessica is blonde and in her thirties. I think she fancies me.'

Sheila laughs down the phone at my comment. 'She feels sorry for you. She probably thinks you're single and too old to meet somebody. What are your plans for tomorrow?'

I cannot remember what I wrote down, so I just say, 'I am going to look at my notes and see what I decided to review first. I have witnesses to examine, friends of the kid who gave a character reference, a baseball cap to use forensics on and that's for starters. I think I will be spending a couple of days going through the list I created. I don't even know if his friends have flown the coop.'

Sheila goes quiet, then says, 'If you find the body, do you want me to do the forensics?'

I can tell that she is feeling close to the case already. 'I think I would prefer that. I want a thorough examination. His body will lead us to the killer.'

Sheila knows that too and tells me, 'Just find the body. I know you are going to do work now before you go to bed, so, I will leave you to it.'

We have been together for so long that we both know how the other thinks. I will be staying up until two o'clock in the morning at least.

THERE IS a spare wall next to the window in the bedroom. My bed is a couple of feet away from the wall, so I roam between the bed and the wall.

During my time as a detective, I would put a horizontal wool string up on a board that acts as a timeline. I would then put people's written statements of events along the string. That always helped me to visualise the time of events.

BEFORE I GET out a ball of wool, I finish my rum and pour another. I wish I had remembered to get ginger ale as I like the sting taken out of the spirit. I will make sure I buy some tomorrow before I get back here.

I STARE at the wall as I pour out a second glass and think how long to have the string. I have six feet to play with.

After I put up five feet of string, I pin the three printed articles up but not along the timeline. I will need to speak to people affected by the incidents and hope they can remember the times.

I take out the contents from the box, except for the cap, and put them on the wall as well. I will wait to speak to the three witnesses to confirm the times on their statements. For now, it is the task of pinning them to the wall next to the three articles.

I check the handwritten notes I made at the police station. My first enquiry is about the three men who saw Daniel coming out of the police station. I think I will spend the day going through their statements.

I am hoping the sheriff or someone will be able to point me in the right direction of where they live or hang out.

Before I find them tomorrow, I carefully read their original statements. I find myself taking a third glass of rum as I stare at the three witness accounts. The first interesting thing is that all three comments are virtually the same. This is odd as they would need to have been interviewed separately so they couldn't collaborate on the same story. It raises alarm bells as they could have been coached to say the lines. It could also mean that they did not see anything and were made to say something.

Without going over the boring details, the three contents are very similar; not from the point of view of telling the same story, but how they told it. The gist of it is that they saw Daniel walk round the corner into the dark.

Each person has a unique way of telling the same story, and each will differ from the others. Based on these notes, the story is written in the same way with the same description which is why it raises concerns for me. Police procedure is to interview people independently so there cannot be any hint of coercion.

I do not suspect James, Marty and Nancy of helping to frame Alex as their stories do place him with Daniel. As I mention before, I want to see the whole picture of what happened on the night.

BY THE TIME I finish with my thoughts, I see it is close to one o'clock in the morning. I finish my fourth glass of rum, feeling abnormally tired from the effects of alcohol.

I change into my pyjamas and go to bed. As I stare at my crazy wall and the story so far, I drift off to sleep.

WEDNESDAY DAY 2

WHEN I WAKE up the next morning, I see it is after seven o'clock and remember that I arranged for Jessica to be here for eight o'clock. I get in the shower straight away before she arrives.

I wonder whether it will be straightforward finding the three men and if they will confess to making up their story.

While I dry myself, I can hear a car engine outside the front of the trailer. I quickly check the time thinking I couldn't have been that long in the shower, but it is only just gone seven forty-five, As I button up my shirt, I hear the door knock and check that I am fully clothed before answering.

When I open the door, Jessica is there holding a couple of small takeaway bags. I show her to the table in the kitchen area.

I attempt to make coffee but don't even know if there is any in the cupboard. I had planned on eating out every day.

Jessica takes two breakfast rolls out of the bags while I still try to find coffee with no success. She is happy to go for coffee after we have our rolls.

While we eat, I notice her observing the tired interior and, eventually, my work on the wall. She walks over to see what I have done.

I watch her reading the statements. 'Do you notice anything suspicious?'

Jessica notices the similarities right away. 'Their accounts of the night seem to be worded the same. Each one should be written independently.'

I expect her to recognise the issue, so I go on, 'What do you think our first port of call is?'

Jessica knows straight away; 'We find these guys and check if their story corroborates.'

We finish eating and head out for coffee first before starting our day. Before we leave, I remember about the videotape and think that I need it converted to a CD.

When we leave the trailer, I notice that my hire car has writing on the door. I then see that the tyres have been slashed.

Jessica is not fazed; 'I noticed that someone had put some paint on it. Assumed you already knew.'

I have a feeling that some people do not want me here. I can just make out the 'N' word spelt wrong with the slogan, 'Leve this town'. That is original when you want to try to scare someone. At least I know the person who wrote it is not educated and dumb. It is a good sign as they are not a threat. I react casually so as not to alarm Jessica and walk over to her car.

It is not my day as I see Justine walking over all smiley. I close my eyes, praying to God that she is not coming to see me. When I open my eyes, I see her waving and I make a half-wave as I still do not know if I'm the one whose attention she is trying to attract.

She continues to wave and eventually comes up to me. 'Morning! Isn't it a lovely day? Is there something wrong?'

Justine notices the car. 'Wow, what happened to your car? Did you park in a bad spot?'

I cannot believe that she thinks this happened outside the trailer park. 'It happened here last night. Was going to ask if you noticed anything.'

Justine reads the paintwork; 'Who is Nigel?'

I wonder if she is joking. 'It is referring to me.'

Justine has a confused look on her face. 'I thought your name was Stoane.'

I cannot believe she is being serious. 'They slashed my tyres as well.'

Justine is not being funny and says, 'I thought someone was playing a practical joke on you.'

I am lost for words and Jessica turns the engine on to hint to Justine that we are leaving now. I use Jessica as an excuse as to why I cannot stay and chat.

Jessica winds down her window as she sees me trying to get rid of Justine and says, 'Come on. We have to get going.'

WHEN WE LEAVE THE SITE, I thank her. We head onto the main road to town, and I mention our first stop, 'I need a tape turned to digital. Can you help with that?'

Jessica knows a store. 'For sure. We can drop that off now and it will be ready by five today. The shop is four doors down from our newspaper.'

I feel relieved, 'Great. For a moment, I thought you were going to say there weren't any stores. That will be a good idea. I need coffee first.'

WHEN WE ARRIVE in the shopping precinct, Jessica parks right outside the digital shop. I ask Jessica to stay in the car. She is not offended and goes on her cell phone while she waits in the car, sipping her coffee. I finish my coffee before I go inside.

It appears closed with the inside lights very low. If the glass door did not have a sign saying open, you would assume it was not trading.

Inside the shop, along the left are three shelves of new digital camcorders for sale. There is a glass cabinet counter along the right housing accessories for the camcorders. There are batteries, additional leads and attachable lenses.

The shop is shallow with a door that takes you to the back. A man is standing behind the counter waiting for me to ask for assistance. He is reading a magazine.

THE MAN behind the counter is Caucasian and appears to be in his early twenties with a developing beard. His hair is brunette, long and scraggly.

The youngster, who is wearing a chequered blue and black shirt, welcomes me. He seems like a technology geek and so it looks promising that he can come up with a solution for restoring the old tape.

. . .

I HAVE the tape in my hand and place it next to his magazine on the counter. 'Can you transfer whatever is on this tape to some form of digital software?'

The man stares at the tape like I have given him a dirty rag. 'What is this? Haha! Only joking. I can put this on a USB. It will take a while.'

I hope he is not thinking days or weeks, so I ask, 'How long?'

The man winces and draws a long breath; 'Maybe a day. Can you wait till five? We close at five-thirty.'

I am relieved and sigh, 'Yes. Will look to get here for five o'clock. Cheers.'

He takes the tape, wondering why I have kept it and now want it watchable.

I almost forget to ask him the price; 'What will this cost?'

The man stares at the tape and studies it. 'I'll do it for twenty dollars.'

I can live with that, so I ask, 'When do you want me to pay?'

The man is laid back and says, 'Pay when you collect.'

With that, I leave the shop and go back to Jessica's car.

12

HOSTILE WITNESSES

During our drive to see the first witness, Jessica suggests going to their local pub. It is their ritual, all three. I feel that they collectively ganged up on Alex. All three have different surnames which, on the outside, would be taken to mean no relation.

I ask Jessica if their statements were ever questioned considering they are related. Jessica tells me that it would not happen today. Things were different back then. I'm even more suspicious of Alex being guilty and supporting his innocence.

It is starting to make me angry that three people, who could be lying, sent him to jail. Jessica can sense my anger and understands why I would be mad. She stays silent which I assume is because she is avoiding upsetting me further.

She tells me that we are going to 'The Feisty Goldfish' bar in West Henderson Street.

WHEN WE ARRIVE, I see it is a square dark beige brick building. I would not have thought that they would come here. It is not a rough pub and not in a poor area.

We park up and go inside to see a clean place and no messy floor. This place attracts nice clientele.

There is the traditional pool table area with four cue sticks on the wall and the triangular frame left on the table.

I assumed that they would be roughnecks based on Jessica's description of them being rednecks. I have to believe that there are creatures of habit here.

The place is quiet considering it is coming up to half-past one. It should be rush hour. I ask Jessica what time they normally come here. All she knows is that they come in here but does not know when.

With Jessica taking the day off work to spend with me and needing to see these witnesses, I suggest staying here. I tell her that we will stay and walk over to the bar. I order a shot of rum for myself and ask her what she would like to drink. Jessica is happy to drink a club soda rather than having to gauge how much she has had to drink to be able to drive.

The man behind the bar is Caucasian with a brown and grey whisker goatee beard and thick wavy hair down to his neck. He is sombre as he looks at me and politely asks what our drinks are.

We have our drink at the bar, and I check my watch anticipating when they will arrive, at least one will be a start. To make the time pass, I ask more about Jessica life living in a town like this.

I ask about her relationship with her dad. 'You two seem to get along well. Surprised your dad did not give you a reference for a job in the city. Has he got a hold on you?'

Jessica eyes tell me that she has regrets. 'My dad insists that I work at the family business. I wanted to get out of this dead-beat town, but never had the courage.'

I wonder what her plans are, so I ask, 'When this case is solved, and you write it up, will you then use your piece to get out of here? Because trust me, you will get picked up.'

Jessica chuckles sarcastically. 'Yeah, right. Not exactly a nationwide story to report.'

I rest my hand on her wrist, 'Trust me. There is a senator, wrong man jailed and a white kid. All the hallmark of a news story scoop. Trust me.'

Jessica does not have faith in my thoughts. 'So, what are going to do when you see them? They are not exactly the social type.'

I think about what she said, and I know I will face hostility.

CLOSE TO TEN O'CLOCK, Jessica and I hear patrons come in and we stop our conversation mid-flow. I motion Jessica to stay where she is and not get involved.

Five men come in and I wait for Jessica to tell me if any of them are James, Nancy and Marty. Jessica tells me that the three of them are here. She describes to me which of the five are the three witnesses I need to talk to.

JAMES APPEARS to be in his sixties which means that he would have been in his twenties as a witness. He dresses like he is still thirty with a baseball cap that a farmer would wear, with a blue and black chequered shirt and ripped sleeves. His jeans are faded blue and ill-fitting with brown worn suede shoes.

He has a pale white face with a short scraggly black beard with grey forming. He is about five feet seven and chubby. His hair is tied up in a ponytail that sticks out from under his cap.

James appears to be the person who calls the shots as he walks in front of them. I assume he coached the other two to make a statement.

MARTY HAS similar clothing to James, but his shirt is dark brown and black with his sleeves torn off.

He is a similar age to James and Nancy with a mullet hairstyle, going bald on top. His face is also pale skinned with stubble.

Marty walks behind him confidently and so possibly may be the next person in line.

NANCY HAS a similar appearance to Marty with the same facial features and so I deduce that they are brothers.

He dresses like the other two with a red and black lumberjack shirt and also has his sleeves removed. He has the same hairstyle as his brother.

I assume that Nancy is younger than Marty and so looks up to his brother.

WE FACE the bar to avoid eye contact and drawing attention to ourselves as we are not regulars. I will have a talk with the three of them after they have bought their drinks and settled down. I want this to be a relaxing interview rather than coming across as hostile.

I order another two drinks and some snacks for us, and I decide to leave it a while before I go up to them. Jessica asks me how I am going to approach them. I tell her that I will quote the senator's and sheriff's names. Then, I will be polite and sincere.

While we are talking, someone comes up behind us and asks me what I am doing in here. Jessica becomes tense and I put my hand on her forearm to make her relax. I assume it is one of the five guys that include James, Marty and Nancy.

When I turn round to see who it is, I see it is one of the witnesses. I see it is James that has come over. He has a grimace on his face like he wants to cause trouble for the sake of it.

I notice Jessica's hands are shaking slightly while I have a confrontation with James. She quietly listens to us.

James asks what I am doing in their bar. 'We don't have you people in here.'

I acknowledge who I am; 'My name is Stoane. Stoane Cold. I am a retired detective. But I can still have you arrested.'

James feels like he is safe in his own little bubble, so he continues, 'You don't frighten me, n____r.'

Jessica is open-mouthed and appalled by his language. It is like she has never heard such horrible language.

I am calm and have dealt with people like him all my life. 'I have come into town to solve the murder of Daniel Harris. You and your two friends lied on paper, and I want to know why.'

James is struggling to compute what I am saying. 'He disappeared. He was not murdered. Alex Jefferson went down for that.'

I ignore his comment and press him; 'I want you to tell me the truth. Or I can get the sheriff to come down here right now and have you, Nancy and Marty flung in jail so fast, it will make your head spin.'

James is still finding it hard to allow his brain to catch up. 'I said your kind is not allowed in here, n____r.'

Jessica almost chokes on her club soda when she hears the 'N' word again.

I feel totally relaxed and not threatened by him at all. 'The correct word is Nubian. My ancestors were Nubian. The word n____r is slang, like pigs for cops. Cops are police officers like Nubians are black people. But I get it. You are intellectually challenged and so you have an excuse for being dumb. Which explains why you lied on your statement about what you saw that night, outside the police station. So, what will it be? Jail, or tell the truth with my friend to record your correct statement?'

Jessica cannot believe how calm I am and how little James intimidates me.

The other four walk over and try to puff themselves up to scare me but it does not shake me.

I ASSESS the five of them and analyse their movements. Their ability to move quickly is very unlikely. They move like sloths. In fact, sloths move faster than them.

My mind thinks about moving Jessica away from harm, then going for James first, then the other four; I will go with the flow.

The other four are holding pool cues. I have already decided what I will do to them. I have to make sure I do not ruin the three witnesses' vocal cords and dominant hands. I also hope I do not break any bones as I do not want to give black people a bad name in this town.

I sense Jessica is beginning to get scared for both of us. I slowly move my left hand towards her in preparation to shove her out of the way.

I am mentally ready to disable all five for the police to come and collect them. I glance at the barman, and he immediately knows to stay behind the bar and gestures his understanding.

James tenses up and I can predict what he is about to do.

I PUT my left arm across Jessica's chest and thrust her back in her chair and hear the chair legs screech.

I watch James try to punch me and I lean back away from him and then grab his forearm. I stand up and swing him around by his arm and let go at full pelt. I see him fly across the room and smash into tables and chairs.

The second person, who is not a witness, swings a cue at me and I hear the swoosh and wind past my ear. He thrashes the cue at me, missing me each time. When I see a chance, I block the cue between my palms and then kick the guy in the balls. He drops instantly and I take the cue away from him and drop it on the floor.

The third scraggly man tries to hit me with his cue thinking he will succeed. I keep my cool and allow my body to flow away from each strike. The moment he misses and hits a brick pillar, I do not hold back and swipe at his jugular with the flat of my hand. He chokes instantly and falls down struggling to breathe.

There is only Marty and Nancy left. They glance at each other and do not try to attack me. They are happy to co-operate with no hostility.

JESSICA STANDS up and walks towards me. 'Where did you learn to fight like that?'

I wind down and collect myself. 'You don't want to know about my past. Let's just say I collected a few unique sets of skills along the way. It entailed retiring early.'

The three men, including James, struggle to get up from the floor and instantly accept defeat.

AFTER ALLOWING them to recover for twenty minutes, Marty, James and Nancy reluctantly speak to me in front of Jessica. I do not get any more unpleasant comments, now they know I can cut their life short.

I direct them to a part of the bar where we will have privacy and no interruptions. I place three chairs in front of a table, like an interview. Jessica and I sit on the other side of the table. I ask her to make notes while I have a casual informal conversation.

I then ask them about their statements from three decades ago with an open question to all three of them. I ask them to answer honestly and stress that I don't care if they never saw anything.

Nancy responds first, hesitantly, 'It was dark when we saw the boy come out of the police station. He walked round the corner.'

I interrupt, 'Yes. You said that the boy disappeared into the dark. Was there anymore to add?'

Nancy shakes his head. 'That is not what we saw. A car pulled up and stopped alongside him. I can't speak for the others, but I did not see who was in the car.'

My eyes light up as I did not see that coming. 'Come again?'

Marty supports his statement, 'We saw the kid get startled. He stood there frozen. After a few seconds, he walked round to the passenger side at the back.'

James adds, 'You have to understand. We were stoned. We were on our last strike. We each had brushes with the law.'

Nancy has remorse on his face as he says, 'We were told that they had a suspect. They wanted us not to screw up the arrest. We were stoned. We assumed that we must have dreamt it. They already had the guy. I have no idea why our account did not fit.'

Jessica is speechless and realises the ramifications; 'So, you cannot say who was in that car.'

James comes over worried as he asks, 'Are we in trouble?'

I tell him honestly, 'Perjury is a crime. Your third strike would have been a couple of months. Do you know what perjury means?'

James goes quiet and shakes his head. 'No.'

I can see they were taken advantage of, so I explain, 'I will find you a lawyer. Just to let you know, you are looking at five years. But that is if you wilfully falsified a statement. I think you were coerced. Forced to have your account fit in with the prosecutor's case.'

Marty is hesitant; 'Are you saying that we sent an innocent man to jail?'

I do not sugar-coat it; 'If the timeline does not fit, then yeah. You made someone spend 37 years in jail. The real killer has had the life of Riley.'

The three of them appear as if they are about to throw up. Something suddenly crosses my mind.

I quickly ask the question before I forget; 'Would you be able to describe the car?'

Nancy is the first to answer; 'It was a sedan car. I think it was black.'

I have an idea. 'If I get a photo of the car, would you remember it?'

Marty is more confident; 'I think I would. If you show me the back of it.'

I want to understand their state of mind, so I ask, 'Were you high or drunk at the time?'

They embarrassingly admit to being there smoking weed to get high. I wonder how they saw anything. I try to make them feel less ashamed of how they are feeling right now. I reassure them that I will find a lawyer for them.

James feels awkward now and asks, 'After how I behaved, why are you helping us?'

I do not mince my words. 'I hate racism in all aspects. I just don't stoop to their level. I have met people who are mentally challenged, and they would not offend anyone. You insult them by behaving like an idiot.'

Jessica tries not to laugh and covers her mouth with her hand. There is nothing else that I need to know. I tell them that I will be seeing them again.

I NEED proper food now and suggest going somewhere else for lunch. It is after midday and Jessica is up for lunch as well.

13

PERCEPTION

We go to 'Bruce's Fabulous Foods' restaurant for lunch. Jessica orders a garden chicken salad and I have a Boursin burger with chips.

Jessica cannot stop thinking about what happened in the bar. 'Where did you learn to fight like that? Don't take it the wrong way but you're not exactly a spring chicken.'

I can see her regressing after her comment, so I explain, 'I spent years learning self-defence in my spare time. It was guerrilla warfare.'

Jessica is impressed. 'Were you not worried about getting hurt or myself being caught up?'

I brush off her comment; 'You train your brain muscle to evaluate your threat and spatial awareness. Before you engage, you think briefly two or three steps ahead of what you know your opponent is going to do. You think worst-case scenario to prepare for everything. It is nothing special. It is simply practicing over and over again.'

Jessica does not think any less of the way I handle those guys and says, 'I am still impressed.'

The conversation changes back to work, and she reminds me about the sedan car.

My mind is already doing overtime; 'We find that car, we get DNA and tie it to Daniel and the killer. I forgot to ask if their timeframe differed. But the video will confirm the time by adding a couple of minutes to when he left the police station. They were stoned anyway and so they would not be aware of time or day.'

Jessica takes out her shorthand notes of my interview. 'They said the car was a black sedan. Doesn't that article you have on the wall match that description?'

I try to visualise the words and picture on the printout. 'I am wondering if the stolen car was used to take Daniel.'

Jessica is beginning to see where I am going, 'Are you saying that we need to find the stolen car and examine it?'

I picture us finding the car. 'Yes. I have an idea how to find it. We can go to the police station tomorrow to locate it. I need to interview Daniel's friends as well. Maybe find where the car is first and then speak to William, Bill and Jack.'

Jessica is on the same wavelength; 'That sounds good. I can find out where they live today. I'm sure they still live in town. No one ever leaves this place.'

I hope so too. 'If we need to take a trip out of town, it will not be an issue.'

Jessica changes the subject briefly and asks, 'Do you want to eat at my parents' home again?'

I am taken aback but say, 'Sure. Only if that will not be a problem.'

Jessica sees that as settled. 'When we are finished, I can take you back to the trailer to freshen up and then drive us to my parents. Then drop you off again.'

I feel like am being a burden; 'Only if that is okay with you. I do not want to put you out of your way. I can get a taxi.'

Jessica brushes the idea off. 'No. Not a problem.'

JESSICA IS BEGINNING to like Stoane as she gets to know him more. She found him sexy when he protected her in the bar. She could not believe how assertively he moved the danger away from her. She puts aside his shiny gold wedding band and imagines what they could be like together.

She wishes that there were people like him living in the town. Jessica wonders why she cannot meet a man like him. She wonders why it has to be someone from out of town. Ideas of imagining his chest under his clothes flow through her mind.

Finally, she decides to suppress her thoughts, keeping herself professional and keeping her friendship distanced.

WE FINISH our lunch and I pay for the bill. It is only just after three o'clock, so I suggest going back to my trailer first to freshen up. Jessica agrees and we head over there.

On our way to the trailer park, I feel Jessica is acting differently towards me. She appears fidgety and I'm not sure why. I hope I have not somehow offended her. She is making less eye contact.

I make menial conversation; 'I'm finding that everywhere is between a five- and eight-minute drive. I didn't think I would make a friend instantly. I thought I would struggle to find someone to assist.'

When we get back to the trailer, we find that we have time to review the stolen car. There is no picture of the stolen car mentioned in the article. We search in the report for a number plate or the make of the car. After a couple of minutes, we find the number plate.

I almost question Jessica about who put this person in charge of this story. However, I hold back as I would be criticising her dad for his choice of reporter.

Jessica moves away from me a couple of times as I try to have a close conversation with her. I assume she has a different perception of me since the confrontation at the bar. She has seen a different side of me which she probably doesn't like.

It is getting close to four forty-five. I quickly go in the shower, so we make it to the shop before it closes.

FROM THE BED, Jessica listens to the sound of Stoane washing himself. She begins to imagine what he is doing in the shower. She thinks about his torso with a film of water cascading over a six-pack. Her mind wanders, imagining her being in the shower with him.

She hears him coming out of the bathroom and quickly jumps onto the bed and lies down. She pretends to be reading a magazine she saw in the bedside drawer.

I WALK in with a bathrobe on, fully covered, to put on fresh clothes for tonight. I notice Jessica is reading an animal magazine. I tell her that I did not figure her to be interested in reading about animals. She is a little surprised when she pushes the magazine away to study the front page.

I choose to pretend that she loves animals when there are none in her parents' house.

Now I am dressed for dinner tonight, we hurry to the camera shop before it closes at five-thirty.

DURING THE DRIVE, I ask more about her. 'Are you dating anyone?'

Jessica reluctantly tells me about her life. 'Everyone is married to their first cousin here. There is no one here who could be a potential.'

I wonder if she has ambition. 'Can you see yourself leaving here and heading to Los Angeles, New York or even abroad?'

Jessica is casual as she answers my question, 'I haven't really thought about it. I'm my own boss to a certain degree. It is chilled out, no 'hold the press' or 'stop the press'. Why would I want to go to a stressed-out job?'

I think she wishes she could leave this life, so I ask her, 'Will you live with your parents all your life?'

Jessica has a faraway look on her face. 'I haven't thought about it. If I was in a relationship, I would want to move out. But that is not going to happen anytime soon.'

Before I know it, Jessica is parking outside the camera shop.

I ASK Jessica to wait in the car while I go inside. I explain that I do not want the guy in the shop to detect that the video is a part of our investigation into the disappearance of the child.

Jessica understands where I am coming from, and she agrees with me. She does not play with her phone this time. She puts the car radio on to listen to music while she waits for me to retrieve the CD.

I WALK to the end of the shop towards the counter and see the man standing there. He holds out something in his hand. I hope it is good news as I do not see the tape and no sign of a digital player.

He shows me a USB stick and pulls the original tape from behind the counter. He babbles about connecting an old VHS player to his computer and playing it through his monitor. Then used the computer recording software to record the video.

My only interest is not in how he did it, but if there is a good copy. He made a point of watching the tape and realised what was on it.

The man places the copy in my hand. 'That is for free. You're here to find the killer?'

I am taken aback by his comment and say, 'How do you know the case? You weren't even born.'

The man seems to know the story. 'I caught snippets of it when I was growing up. It was the talk of the town for years. Everyone had a theory. No one seems to care about his disappearance stroke murder. Do you think the guy who got arrested didn't do it?'

I understand where he is coming from. 'That is what I am here to find out. He won't say because he doesn't know and hence why he has been pleading his innocence all these years.'

The man wants reassurance. 'Will you find the boy's real killer?'

I have confidence that I will find the boy's body, so I can promise, 'I will get to the truth of what happened, regardless of where it takes me.'

I thank him for the conversion and warn him that I may need more video-tapes converted. He is more than happy to help and do it for free. I tell him how much I appreciate it. He asks me to let him know when I solve the mystery. I tell him to read it in the paper.

DURING OUR DRIVE to her home, Jessica is not talkative. That is fine with me as my mind is wondering what could be on this USB.

I am grateful for the five-minute drives around this town.

DINNER IS JUST as wonderful as last night with similar provisions. Our conversations turn to my thoughts of the town.

'I have been to a couple of restaurants now. The staff are friendly and welcoming. I find the customers discretely staring at me. There is a term called covert racism. It means that people do not openly say they are prejudiced. My hire car also got redecorated and the tyres slashed.'

Tony is surprised; 'I'm sorry you experienced that. But for the quiet stares, unfortunately, people know why you are here. News travels; it is likely they see you as a celebrity. It is more likely they were star-struck.'

I feel awkward now. 'What are the people really like here?'

Tony is honest and tells me, 'Folks have come a long way since 1982. People are more culturally knowledgeable. We are not in a bubble. We have more tourists and visitors coming through. Back then, we were like an isolated village. Any new face seemed strange.'

I think of Alex back then and ask, 'Is that why you thought he was innocent? He did not get a fair trial because of his skin?'

Tony replies to the contrary; 'No. Just looking at how the case was developing; I knew something was not quite right. I could not see how they linked Alex to the disappearance. The evidence they had seemed too thin. But I could not disprove it.

Patricia gives her thoughts; 'He would come home every night discussing new developments in the case. Seeing his notes also made me think he was innocent. But no one would pay attention to us. He was just reporting the news.'

I ask Tony if he has kept his notes on the case and he shows me to his study. He has it stored in one of the desk drawers in a foolscap folder. I ask if I can borrow it in case there is something I can use.

After he gives me the folder, I feel the need to go home and think about watching the video on the USB stick.

Jessica offers to take me back and tells her parents not to wait up.

14

REPLAY

We park up outside my trailer. Jessica has not said a word on the way here. During the drive, I could not stop thinking about what could be on the USB.

WHEN WE GO INSIDE, Jessica brings with her a laptop she borrowed from home to see what is on the USB.

I grab a washed glass from the draining board and pour out some rum. As I go to drink, I see Jessica watching me in anticipation. I take the hint and put my glass down to pour her one.

We sip our drinks together as we make eye contact. We both gulp down the whole glass of rum together. We gently smile at each other, and I pour out another two glasses of rum. Then we go to the laptop to turn it on.

I WAIT IMPATIENTLY for the screen to come alive, so the USB can be plugged in. We feel anxious to see this video.

Jessica pushes the stick into the side of the laptop, and it takes a few seconds for the computer to open the content.

A media software icon automatically pops up in the middle of the screen with the play symbol. I move my finger across the mouse touchpad to make the cursor move over to the media software, then tap and the video begins playing.

INITIALLY, the video shows the empty lobby area of the police station. I check the time stamp in the bottom left of the video, to compare it with the three men's revised witness statements. The time on the tape so far is seven o'clock in the evening. The three men were too stoned to know the exact time they saw Daniel get in the car.

Jessica is standing close to me, and I can smell her aroma which is pleasant. It almost distracts me from noticing Daniel walk into view of the camera. I quickly check the time to see that it is a little after seven now and I watch him walk up to the counter. Jessica is poised like me to see what will unfold in the tape.

A moment later, the child goes to sit down and wait for someone. Based on the time he sat down and when he suddenly left, he waited for about five minutes.

There is nothing else to see in the video, so I get us another glass of rum. I realise that Jessica is not going to be able to drive home tonight, but I am happy for her to stay over to analyse what we know so far. Jessica is happy to take the glass from me and continue drinking.

I think out loud, 'There is something not right here. You walk into a police station. You ask to speak to an officer. You are told to sit down and wait for someone to see you. Then, after only five minutes, you just walk out. You don't have the patience to wait. Does that seem right to you?'

Jessica sips a few times, 'Let's play devil's advocate. You go in and ask to speak to someone. It is getting late. You are a kid and need to be home for a certain time. It is passing your curfew. You cannot wait any longer. You need to be getting home now.'

I walk back and forth with my drink. 'Okay, he has a curfew. What child doesn't? But should you be home by six o'clock, not seven? Be home before it gets dark. It was already dark after five o'clock. The curfew doesn't play into this. Run the tape again. From when he sits down to wait.'

I watch her lean over to replay the video and notice for the first time that she has a nice rear. A pleasing shape. Then, my wife pops into my head and I start to think that she could be my eldest child if I had her in my early twenties.

I walk over to see the replay and the five seconds of walking away bugs me. There is something niggling me. I keep asking her to replay the short footage. I can see her getting tired of seeing the same scene for the tenth time. I humour her by asking her to replay it for an eleventh time, but I ask her to pause it immediately. That is, it. I can see what is bugging me. The child is staring past the officer at the counter. Someone in the back office is there and the boy sees someone who startles him. I explain this to Jessica, but she is struggling to see what I see.

I circle the boy's head with my forefinger. 'Focus on his head. Play back the tape. Just focus on what his head is doing.'

Jessica studies what I'm pointing at then says, 'You're right. Something in the back room spooked him. We need the camera that films inside the office. We need to check that tape at precisely 7.09.'

We feel we have made a breakthrough and celebrate like one of us got a promotion. I find us hugging each other.

OUR EYES LOCK, and, for a brief second, I feel us coming closer and feel Jessica's lips near mine. We realise what is about to happen and both pull away feeling embarrassed. We both sober up quickly and Jessica downs her remaining rum. We feel awkward around each other and make small talk.

AFTER OUR NERVES CALM DOWN, I suggest we go to bed but correct myself with going to sleep separately.

Jessica is still shocked with herself and stays quiet, nodding her head in agreement. I go to get changed in the bathroom and allow her to get ready in the bedroom.

WHEN I COME BACK IN, I imagine her being only in her underwear hoping that it is only in my head. I notice her in my bed on the far side next to the wall.

I decide to call my wife before going to bed and have a conversation at the back of the trailer, so I do not wake her.

Our conversation is about our respective days, and I do not mention that I have a woman staying in my trailer. I only stay on the phone for ten minutes and then eventually fall asleep on top of the duvet after midnight.

I occasionally wake up thinking that Jessica is lying against me.

THURSDAY DAY 3

THE NEXT MORNING, I wake up and remember that Jessica almost kissed me last night. I'm not sure if I encouraged her or it just happened. I wonder if this is going to ruin our working relationship. I need her as a guide in this town to help me around. It will save time trying to find where I need to be.

I gently roll over to see if she is awake without disturbing her. When I face her, all I see an empty space on that side of the bed. She is not there.

I jump out of bed to see if she is still here or whether she was embarrassed and decided to avoid me. I check to see if the bathroom door is locked and also the toilet. She is nowhere to be seen.

As I come to the conclusion that she cannot face me, I hear the front door open, and Jessica walks in with a smile. She has hot drinks and breakfast again and is wearing fresh clothes.

WHILE WE EAT our breakfast in the kitchen, she behaves like last night never happened. I do not know whether to make closure or follow her lead by not acknowledging the elephant in the room.

Jessica is excited about finding out who startled Daniel. She assumes this will lead us to the person who could actually have murdered him instead of Alex Jefferson.

While we have our breakfast, we place her laptop on the table as well. I go through the video again and focus more on his clothing and imagine where he could have been. I can see he is wearing a light blue shirt with a white T-Shirt underneath and a pair of typical blue jeans of that era.

I notice his jeans have ingrained dirt on his knees which tells me he had been into the woods. It also opens up a new avenue to discovering what he did before he came to the police station. I need to know where he went.

Jessica finds the way my brain is wired fascinating and would never have thought of studying why Daniel's clothes were messy. Also, she is amazed at Daniel knowing someone who works in the police station and who also scared him.

I mention that today, I will be finding the three friends Daniel hung around with to build up a picture of how he lived.

Jessica knows where two of them live and is not sure about the third person. I also want to ask the three, now men, where they socialised as kids. I feel this is crucial to solving where he died and how. She is beginning to realise why I show an interest in a victim's previous life.

Jessica also mentions that we need to ask for more videotapes of the camera facing the back office. I agree and suggest that we go to the police station after seeing the three men.

As we finish our coffees, she asks me when I will see Daniel's parents. I make it clear that I never speak to the victim's parents as their character witness statements are always biased. I explain that I want an honest view, regardless of whether or not it is in a positive light. It helps me to work out how the person allowed themselves to put their life in harm's way.

Jessica suddenly remembers the information she has; 'Oh, I thought I would proactive. I went on the electoral roll to search the three boys. William Jackson is now an accountant and I found out where he works. Bill Walker has no known address. So, I'm hoping William or Jack will know where he is. Jack Hall is a lawyer and I also know where he is working.'

I like how organised she is; 'That's great. Nothing like the present.'

· · ·

WE GO to the first person, William Jackson, who works at an accountancy firm. He does not know that we are going to visit him. I do not want to give him a heads up, so he does not have a chance to think about his responses. I want a first opinion of his thoughts.

I also think about calling my friend Trudy who is in forensics as I will want her to test samples from the cap. Also, I will need her to carry out any other tests on whatever evidence we may find from here on in.

TRUDY MILLAR IS a black African American woman in her forties. She is five feet six with a pear-shaped body and dark flawless skin. Her face is round and filled out with long afro curls to her shoulder.

Her personality is happy-go-lucky, and she is career-focused, taking her vocation very seriously. Outside of work, she is the life and soul of the party and enjoys her drink and food. But her colleagues would not think so by the way she conducts herself at work.

She is single with no sign of a boyfriend on the horizon. She loves her role and cannot think of any other career. But she is content with her life and wants for nothing.

She has a couple of nieces who are not much older than the boy who is the cold case. So, it is close to her heart to help Stoane give peace to the boy's parents.

She works for the New York Police Department in Crime Scene Investigation. She has been there since she graduated and worked her way up to Supervisor.

JESSICA DRIVES us to the 'Marion Community Tax Services' firm.

A NEW LIGHT

We arrive in reception at the practice firm and ask for William. Their secretary is a woman in her sixties with a cream and white plaid two-piece suit skirt. Her soft voice calls him to see two people interested in a re-opened case.

Jessica and I can hear his voice coming through on the call. He sounds matter of fact and is not fazed by our presence.

We sit down on a sofa in the reception area while we wait for him to come.

A few moments later, he appears and has no hint of why we are here or why I have asked to see him.

William is in business mode, expecting us to ask for his professional services and technical advice. His persona changes from night to day when he realises that we are here for the Daniel Harris case.

I suggest that we go somewhere else and have this discussion away from work.

WE TAKE William in the car and suggest seeing this interview as a working lunch. I explain that I have general questions to ask to find out more about what Daniel's personality had been like. I put him at ease by saying that my line of questioning is nothing about him. I also say that he is not in trouble and there is no new line of enquiry. I explain that I have been asked to find out where Daniel is and find answers to what happened.

JESSICA DRIVES us to a sparse car park with a burger van open for lunch. I ask what William and Jessica would like and then go and buy our lunch a little before eleven o'clock.

When I come back with each person's choice of lunch, Jessica and I stay in the front of the car, so it feels like more of a formal enquiry.

I ask about his relationship with Daniel first. 'How close were you two?'

William is curious, 'We hung out as friends with two others.'

I hazard a guess, 'That would be Bill and Jack? You three gave a character witness statement. Tell us what your typical play day was like.'

William is baffled and asks, 'Don't you want to know about Daniel?'

I want to know Daniel's routine, so I say, 'We will get to that. I want to know what you did as kids.'

William reminisces, 'We went to our favourite hangout every day after school without fail.'

I interrupt him, 'Where did you go?'

William talks about their favourite place. 'There is a clearing in the woods that we played in. There is a tree we used to climb. We could never get to the top of the tree trunk. We dared Daniel for a dollar to climb the tree to the top. He did it and fell down spraining his wrist.'

I picture his childhood, 'Can you take us there? Now?'

William is reluctant as he needs to get back to work and asks, 'How will going there solve his disappearance?'

Jessica jumps in; 'We can learn about his habits, and it will probably help us to understand what he was doing.'

William sighs and takes his cell phone out and tells his colleagues he is going to be out of the office for the rest of the day.

WILLIAM DIRECTS Jessica to the woods where the four boys played and climbed the tree. Jessica has an idea where he could be taking us as she finds the area familiar.

The road we take is quiet and makes me think that anything could happen here, and no one would know. There would be no witnesses.

William tells Jessica to slow down, and I assume we are not far now. She begins to turn left into an off-beat road called 'Cove Forest Road'. Eventually, we stop at the edge of the forest opening, a few feet away.

WILLIAM APPEARS apprehensive as I can see in his face, he is thinking back to being six years old again. Jessica and I let William lead the way as we follow him through the short grass for a couple of minutes. The ground is wide with trees and foliage on either side of us.

He says that he has not been here since his best friend went missing. He did not think that his emotions would heighten as he walks us to his old stomping ground.

When we reach the spot where the four of them played around, there is no one around and you can hear a pin drop.

The tree William talked about is still here but no longer alive. There are no leaves, and the trunk and branches are dried out to almost a beige colour. The bark is like a reptile's skin and partly flaked off.

WILLIAM DESCRIBES how the place originally appeared back in 1982. He explains that the ground around us used to be worn like bare carpets with dusty mud. It now has an inch of grass covering the area.

I notice a path on the other side of the area. 'Where does that path lead?'

William has a blank face; 'I don't know. We never went beyond this spot. Just played and made our own fun.'

I turn to Jessica and ask, 'Do you know?'

Jessica shrugs, 'Nope.'

I feel that the path is beckoning me to walk down there to see where it takes us. 'Another day, we will have to take a walk down there.'

William remembers something, 'There is one thing that I did not tell the police. I didn't think it was relevant at the time. Also, I felt intimidated being so young.'

I hurry him along; 'Spit it out.'

William hesitates, then says, 'One day, Daniel was curious about venturing along that path. The rest of us were not interested. It was never mentioned again.'

I have one more question; 'Did he have an inquisitive mind? Looking for trouble?'

William thinks back; 'Yes. He did like to snoop around.'

Jessica takes some notes down as she remembers to report any new findings. I ask him where I can find Bill and Jack. He tells me that Jack is a lawyer and works at 'Timothy Cole Attorney At Law'. Bill has no address as he goes from town to town. But he does have a cell phone and William has his number.

I decide that the next move is to talk to Jack as I know where he is. I ask William to take us to his office.

We go back to the car to head to the law firm. Jessica knows how to get there. William wants to come along to further help with building a profile of Daniel.

During the drive there, I cannot stop thinking about that path and at some point, taking a walk to see if it can help in the case.

WHEN WE ARRIVE, William suggests going to a bar to continue my enquiry. William already called Jack to say that we were on our way.

He is stood outside his firm waiting for us. The bar is within walking distance, and it happens to be lunchtime. Jack tells us that he has taken the afternoon off to talk to us.

THE BAR HAS MORE patrons than the previous one we visited. We are greeted by a waitress who shows us to a table to have drinks and some food.

It is a contemporary establishment with nice cutlery and a menu to choose from. Jessica and I go ahead with ordering.

While waiting for our lunch, I ask Jack a little about himself. 'What do you remember about Daniel?'

Jack changes his mind and takes a menu. 'I don't know why you are asking. I gave them the same information back in 1982. How can supplying the same information make anything different? The cops never found him back then. What on earth can you do differently that the police didn't already do?'

I do not explain my methods but give him reassurance, 'I work differently. I don't like relying on old witness statements. They never solved the original crime. So, I like to review cases my own way. So, please answer my questions. What do you remember of your Daniel?'

Jack relaxes and begins, 'He liked playing a detective. He would look for something that wasn't there. He was fixated with wanting to be a detective.'

William appears surprised. 'I didn't know that he wanted to be a cop. I thought he just enjoyed pretending.'

Jack seems to have a different fondness for their best friend; 'If he had not put his nose in other people's business, he would still be here. He would still be with us.'

I can see he has never moved on from that night. 'It was not your fault. If it was not that night, it would have been another time. You would not have been able to prevent it.'

William directs the conversation back onto Daniel's character; 'We're not here to dwell on how he could go missing. We're here to help the detective build up a profile of the victim.'

Jack apologises and thinks back to his childhood. 'Daniel did not create any enemies. We were regular kids. We did not find trouble or get into trouble. Everyone liked him. And there was no curb crawler if that is what you're thinking. This is a small town. Everyone knows each other. And Daniel would never talk to strangers. We shared everything. So, if he got himself into trouble, he would have come to us for help. He would never try to deal with the problem by himself.'

I find his comments helpful. 'You have no idea how that helps me. You see, you never mentioned this before to the cops, so, it always helps to get a fresh pair of ears.'

Jack almost laughs at my sense of humour. 'Anything else?'

I want to know more about his state of mind, so I say, 'You said he would never deal with a problem by himself. You never noticed anything strange about him? He didn't act differently on the days leading up to his disappearance?'

Jack shakes his head. 'No. If there was, trust me, we would have dragged it out of him. We never kept secrets.'

I have one more question. 'Had you ever seen Alex Jefferson before? Did he hang out where you played? Ever notice him staking you guys out?'

William answers confidently, 'No. A black man? He would have stood out like a sore thumb. Which is what we found strange. We never knew of him until the police arrested him. I thought it was kind of stupid to leave his cap in his guest house. If you were going to murder someone, you wouldn't leave something obvious to implicate yourself.'

I find this kind of conversation refreshing. 'Now, you're thinking. You wonder if Daniel would have thought like this if he were around? Let's just agree that Alex Jefferson is guilty. To make things simple. He wouldn't tell me when I saw him four days ago.'

William and Jack are open-mouthed after I tell them. I see what Jessica's reaction is and she cannot believe it herself.

William has questions to ask. 'Did he confess to kidnapping him? Killing him? Did he give you a clue where Daniel is?'

I reach out with my hands to wave him to calm down. 'I saw him before I arrived in town. He still protests his innocence. He sticks to the same story that he was with someone else. I believe him. I read his eyes and facial expression. But that is between us four. I have not told anyone up till now. Whether you believe me or not, I am not going to argue with you. Now, there is another problem. He is going to be executed at some point, which gives me limited time to solve Daniel's disappearance. There is no evidence to prove Alex didn't do it. The only proof is finding the person who did do it.'

Jack has hope in his eyes as he asks me, 'Will you tell us before everyone else? I want to look them in the eye and ask why.'

I cannot make any promises, so I insist, 'I will do the asking. I don't want you to regret ruining your career.'

William is intrigued as to how I will solve the mystery. 'What plan do you have?'

I have an idea but do not want to disclose it. 'If I tell you, there will be a risk of the plan failing.'

When we finish our lunch, we walk to the car park at Jack's office and then Jessica and I drive William back to his office.

.   .   .

JESSICA PARKS OUTSIDE THE OFFICE. I remind William that I need him to call Bill to have the same kind of conversation. William is more than happy to put him in touch with us. I ask if he can have him come to my trailer to save time, on the assumption that he is not far from the town.

William is confident that he can get him to come over to my trailer.

After dropping William off, Jessica drives us back to my trailer to review the notes that she made. Before we do get there, I suggest that I finally buy coffee and milk to keep in the trailer and some food for breakfast at least.

She drives me to a supermarket that is still open to allow me to shop for essentials.

WHEN WE GET BACK to my trailer, I make us coffee and open a packet of biscuits to go with it. We sit at the table and go over the notes she made from the conversations with both William and Jack.

As she reads out her notes of the two interviews, I conjure up a picture in my head of who Daniel could have seen. I tell Jessica that we know he had an inquisitive mind. Therefore, Daniel may have found a new entity to investigate, but not knowing it would cost his life.

Jessica is agreeing with me and also came to the same conclusion independently. She wants to enquire about the stolen car after we finish talking to Bill. I wonder who is leading this case.

JESSICA IS TRYING to impress Stoane by anticipating his next move and coming up with the idea first before he does. Her head has shut off her feelings from growing further for him. But her heart continues to fight to the surface. She cannot help herself staring longingly into his eyes and wondering what he would be like in bed.

Last night, she struggled to sleep and found herself watching him quietly sleeping. She imagined herself reaching under the sheets towards his pyjama bottoms, stirring him from sleep as she massaged him.

IT IS COMING CLOSE to five o'clock and I assume she will be ready to head back home. I will not spend the evening at her parents' home a third time as I want to focus on tomorrow's itinerary.

I want to search for the stolen car reported in the newspaper back in 1982. I also want to phone Trudy in preparation for using her forensic skills. Finally, I want to call Sheila to see how her day has been and give her the rundown on today's events.

Jessica does not seem to be in a hurry to leave when I casually say the time, expecting her to take the hint.

Even if I were not married, I would not take advantage of someone half my age. Jessica deserves to have a fling or an affair with someone her own age. I have no interest in having an affair when I have fulfilment in my life. I find her attractive and can understand someone else being happy to ruin their marriage for a one-minute fling, but I have no interest.

I also have respect for her from the point of view that she should be experience intimacy with a boyfriend, not having to rely on a married man as a substitute.

To avoid any awkwardness, I organise tomorrow's day as a distraction and also to keep our relationship professional.

I want to see Bill in the morning and then spend the late morning, early afternoon tracing the stolen vehicle. I have a hunch and want to prove or disprove that. I also want to call Trudy to come here and begin helping in the forensic tests on the baseball cap and anything else.

If William does not contact me tonight, I will chase him up tomorrow and force the meeting with Bill.

While discussing this with Jessica, I write my thoughts down with rough times and my perception of how long it will take to locate the car.

One final arrangement is to find the video that is facing the back office of the police station, particularly at the time when Daniel gave a startled reaction and left the station. I want to know who the admin worker or police officer was.

I notice Jessica gazing at me while I go through a structured itinerary on paper. I blank her while I reiterate what I have mentioned. I abbreviate the plan saying that we will interview Bill, search for the stolen car and call Trudy to make her way here.

It is coming up to seven o'clock now and there is nothing else I need to discuss. I have two phone calls to make now. I will call Trudy first and then my wife.

I use this as an excuse to be direct and ask her to leave so I can make some phone calls and cook myself a meal.

Jessica respects my privacy and realises that her parents will be expecting her home for dinner now.

After she leaves, I hear my cell phone sound and see that William has confirmed via a text that the meeting with Bill is at ten o'clock tomorrow at my trailer.

16

OUR FIRST BREAK

Friday Day 4

JESSICA IS punctual arriving at eight o'clock again. She asks how the rest of my evening went and how my wife is.

I tell her that we are missing each other, and she may be interested in coming down to spend time together. I can see on her face that she is accepting that I am not freely available.

She asks me about Trudy in regard to how I know her and what she does for a living. I explain that she is a forensic scientist and I've known her for years from when I used to be a detective.

I mention that I have asked her to come down at short notice when I have evidence to analyse. I do not want her to make a single trip to analyse the baseball cap alone.

I also mention that William texted last night to say that Bill is coming to us this morning for ten o'clock.

WHILE WE WAIT for his appearance, I make a bacon sandwich and ask if she has eaten yet. She accepts my offer of making her one too while she makes us coffee.

During breakfast, she asks me how I will track down a car from thirty-eight years ago. Without getting into the technical side of things, I tell her that there is a database that keeps records of all makes and models. All we have to do is input a number plate which we have from the article I printed from her office. Jessica is impressed with my method but assumes the car will have been crushed at some scrap yard. I, on the other hand, feel that it will be lying around untouched. It is one of my hunches.

BILL ARRIVES PROMPTLY at ten o'clock, nervous and apprehensive as if he is going to be in trouble. I offer him a drink and wonder if he needs food. I wonder when he last had a full meal. I automatically make him a hearty meal even though it is early for lunch.

Jessica puts him at ease by sitting with him at the table having coffee with him. She makes small talk asking where he is living and how often he stays in touch with William and Jack. I hear him telling her that he moves around and never stays long in one place. He never moved on after his best friend went missing.

He is grateful for me providing baked chicken with rice and frozen vegetables. As soon as I finish cooking, I get a plate and take out the food.

I SIT down with them and wait for Bill to eat first and feel ready to talk. By the way he quickly feeds himself, I can see he has not had a decent meal for a while. I do not want to interrupt his enjoyment of eating a home-cooked meal.

He has an untidy beard, and his hair is hidden under a grubby yellow woolly hat. His eyes are sunken in, and his skin is weathered.

AFTER HE FINISHES CLEARING the plate, I can now begin asking the same questions as I asked the other two.

I wait for Jessica to get her notepad and pen ready. 'What do you remember about Daniel?'

Bill gathers his thoughts before saying, 'He was inquisitive about activities where we hung out. He wanted to know everything that was happening in our neighbourhood.'

I have something niggling me about his persona; 'Did something happen that makes you feel guilty or remorseful?'

Bill almost breaks down with emotion as he thinks back. 'I was the last person to see him.'

I stare at Jessica in surprise and ask him to elaborate. 'Tell me, how was he behaving?'

Bill takes his time composing an accurate description. 'I was watching a well-known children's cartoon called "Batfink". He came round to ask me to go with him on a stakeout. He really wanted me to go with him. But all I could think about was my cartoon. If I had just gone that day, he would be here now.'

Jessica and I watch him break down in tears and we allow him time to compose himself. I would imagine that if he had gone with Daniel, both of them would have disappeared.

I wonder if he knew where Daniel was going, so I ask, 'Do you know who he was going to spy on or where he was going?'

Bill wishes he knew. 'I didn't ask, and he didn't tell me what he was surveilling.'

'Give me a description of your friend,' I prompt Bill.

Bill thinks about what he always had with him and says, 'He would carry with him a camera and a black notebook. Without fail. He would never go without it.'

I think back to the video. 'I do not remember seeing him with a camera or a black notebook in the video of his last movements.'

Bill is adamant; 'I know that he carried his notebook with him for reporting suspicious activities. He would have taken photos of what he observed as evidence and a reminder. He never went without them.'

I need to know how he carried the items; 'Could you explain how he carried his camera and where he kept his notebook?'

Bill uses his arms to help him remember. 'He kept his book in his jeans pocket, but his camera was round his neck.'

I visualise Daniel on the tape and try to remember if I noticed his camera around his neck. It is not clear if he had his notebook in his pocket.

I think out loud, 'Those two items would have been taken by the suspect. They would have been kept with the cap. It is looking more and more like Alex was telling the truth. His accommodation would have been taken apart. If he did hide them somewhere else, then why be inconsistent and keep the baseball cap?'

Bill agrees. 'If I was going to kidnap somebody, I would make sure there was no sign of them. I'd keep everything with them. I would not take an item of clothing from them. I would have destroyed the camera and notebook as evidence implementing me. I would make sure there was no evidence of him.'

There is nothing else I need to know, so I ask if there is anywhere, he needs to go. His mind is slow as he thinks about the question. Jessica suggests taking him to his parents' house, but he quickly dismisses the idea. He makes his own way out of the trailer park, and I wonder where he is going to go next.

AFTER BILL LEAVES, we summarise Jessica's notes and then place them on the wall with the other five interviews.

The first step is now complete - we have gone over James, Nancy, Marty,

William, Jack and Bill's statements. Their versions are much better than the statements made back in 1982, which is why I needed to speak to them myself rather than relying on their original interviews.

The next move is to have the baseball cap examined using the latest forensic technology. But I need Trudy here as I know she is very thorough. I give her a quick call.

Trudy answers straight away. 'Hi. Long-time, no hear. Why are you calling now? I thought you were busy writing books.'

I smile at her chirpy voice and say, 'I wish. I have been given a cold case to work on. I am in Marion, North Carolina. I need your help.'

Trudy is more than happy to help. 'What do you want me to do?'

I mention a few things; 'I have a baseball cap that needs to be examined. But I have a hunch and I'm about to track it down. If I find what I am looking for, I will want that examined as well. So, it will be a few days.'

Trudy sees this as work-related. 'I will tell my boss that the police department wants my assistance. Get this on police time. Have my expenses paid for. How soon do you want me down there?'

I am pleased that she can drop everything at a moment's notice and tell her, 'Great. Can you come down in two days? That will give me time to locate a car so you can do forensic testing on that.'

Jessica is surprised to hear my theory while I talk to my friend.

Trudy is intrigued by my case. 'What are you up to? I thought you gave up your badge to write.'

I am conscious of Jessica listening to my conversation. 'I did turn to writing. Wrote a couple of books. Then my wife got sick of me moping around the house. So, I was going for a job interview before I had three cop cars drag me to a senator. I now have a thirty-nine-year-old case to solve.'

Trudy is excited now. 'You're kidding! I'll tell my boss that I need to be down there tomorrow. I can use some equipment here and bring them down with me.'

Before hanging up, I ask her about her home life and if she has met someone yet. She is still unattached but happy with her life.

Soon after finishing the phone call, Jessica and I head to the police station.

ON OUR WAY THERE, Jessica brings up the conversation I had with Trudy. In particular, visiting Alex before coming into town.

Jessica is surprised that I saw him in prison. 'What did you talk about?'

I tell her honestly, 'I asked him directly if he did it. He still denied doing it. I then asked about his alibi and still would not give me his source. I read the micro-expressions on his face, and I could see he was telling the truth. Despite believing him, something is bothering me about his alibi.'

'What do you find suspicious about his unidentified source?'

I cannot put my finger on it, so I just say, 'I am thinking that the person does not want their identity known. So, put pressure on him not to say. I know he was sleeping with them. Only love would make him protect them.'

Jessica is in agreement; 'If you were facing jail, you would not sacrifice yourself for anyone. Do you know who it could be?'

'I am trying to figure that out.'

Jessica changes the subject; 'What were you talking about in regard to a book?'

I do not feel comfortable discussing this, so I say, 'Nothing really. I had an idea about using forensics to help detectives to understand a victim's last-known whereabouts. So, analysing samples that their clothes pick up outdoors. Samples such as soil, leaves, pollen and so on. Rather than just the crime scene.'

Jessica assumes that I have written books on it. 'I assume you wrote a theory on it. How many have you published?

I feel awkward mentioning it but admit, 'I may have written six books on it.'

Jessica is fascinated by my theory. 'That probably explains why people here are staring at you funny. They probably realise you are a celebrity.'

I shrug it off, saying, 'They know I am investigating the disappearance of Daniel and are itching to ask me how the search is going.'

Jessica thinks differently; 'I reckon they did a web search on you and found out about you being an author.'

I chortle, brushing it off.

WHEN WE REACH the police station, we use one of their computers to locate the stolen vehicle. We will soon find out if the car is still being driven or has been scrapped.

Their system is linked across the country and so we can see where the sedan has ended up. I can also find out who owned the vehicle and ask them what they remember.

A few minutes later, we find out where the last known address is. Jessica can find our way there. As we go to leave, Bob comes out of his office for an update.

I tell him that we have finished interviewing the original witnesses and are now following a hunch. He asks about the video and whether I have learnt anything new. I mention that the kid recognised someone in the office. That reminds me to ask him for copies of videos relating to the camera that faces the office. Bob has disappointing news that there will be no other video-tapes from 1982. Their policy back then was to tape over them after a month until they were worn out. So, I will not be able to find out who startled Daniel.

I have an idea how to find out who that person could have been, but that is for another day, when we find Daniel's body.

In the meantime, we head to the address where the car is held.

17

CLOSER TO THE TRUTH

We arrive in North Garden Street where the car should be. The area is very leafy with thick trees camouflaging the properties.

The car is a 1970 black Chevy Camaro and has been owned by one person. We park outside the house of the owner.

The owner of the car is a man by the name of Mark Dermot. The newspaper article did mention his name but for obvious reasons, not his address.

THE HOUSE IS MEDIUM-SIZED; I'm guessing it is a four-bedroom house. It has a large front lawn that is weathered by the sun with a path leading to the house. The house has grey wooden slats with wooden windows matching the same colour.

Jessica and I walk up to the front door of the house. I check to see if the car is in the drive, but it is not in sight.

I ring the doorbell and wait for the owner or a member of the family to answer. A moment later, an elderly man comes to the door. He is very slim with short white hair and has a slight hunch. He is almost six feet tall wearing a pair of chinos, a shirt and an open cardigan. I assume it is Marks's dad or another relative.

I introduce us, 'Hi. My name is Stoane, and my colleague is Jessica. We are looking into a cold case to find out what happened back in October 1982. Around that time, I believe that Mark reported his car stolen. Is he here?'

The man is obviously concerned. 'I'm his father. Why are you interested in a crime that happened forty years ago?'

I put him at ease; 'You can call the sheriff if you like. You can call him now while we wait.'

He does not make the call. 'It's okay. Come in.'

HE OPENS the door wider and allows us to come in. I let Jessica walk in first and he leads us into his living room.

He motions us to sit down together on his sofa and offers us refreshments. I follow Jessica's lead whether to say yes to a drink. Jessica asks for a coffee and so I follow suit asking for coffee also.

After he comes back with the coffees, he is happy to talk to us without validating our credentials.

Before I discuss anything, I ask for his name and he tells me it is James.

I begin with his account of events; 'I would like to thank you for your time, James. Where is your wife? Is she out?'

James slouches in his armchair, 'She died a few years ago.'

I show my compassion, 'I'm sorry to hear that. How long were you married?'

James happily tells us, 'We were together for fifty-five years. She died of Alzheimer's. Are you two married?'

Jessica is quick to reply, 'No. I could only dream of being with someone for that long.'

I feel for him; 'I have been married for only twenty years. Married late in life. Can you remember back in 1982?'

James ponders on my question, 'Are you recording this?'

I respond honestly, 'Jessica is a reporter for the local town newspaper. She will be taking notes during this time. Were you there when the car was stolen?'

James slowly recalls that night; 'It was my son who recognised his car being broken into. I was busy watching my tv programme. By the time Mark got outside to see who it was, they had already broken into the car and went skidding out of the drive. I told the police all about this.'

I smile at his annoyance. 'Your report was not included in the cold case I am working on. I am checking to see if your son's account of events is related to it. Please go on.'

James continues, 'When I heard my son shouting outside, I quickly rushed out to see what the commotion was all about. I could barely make out three men in the car.'

I raise my eyebrows as I recall my interview with the three men. 'Can you say that again?'

James repeats his statement with agitation, 'My son told the cops that he thought there were three guys in the car. He assumed that they were joyriders looking for excitement on Halloween Night.'

I turn to Jessica in hope that the two incidents are linked together. I can see from her face she is trying to hide her excitement.

I keep my composure and finish some more questions; 'Are you sure there were possibly three people in that car?'

James gets a little frustrated with my responses; 'I just told you that my son saw three men in the car. If he says that's what he saw, then that is what happened.'

I have one final question; 'Can you tell me what happened to the car?'

James is dithering with an answer; 'He kept it for a few years and then ended up buying a family car. He met someone and had kids. It was not practical anymore.'

I sigh and get frustrated. 'The Department of Motor Vehicles said that the car was still registered here.'

James almost goes into a daze when he stares out of the window. 'He wanted to keep it, but his partner didn't. So, he gave it to me.'

I light up with optimism as I ask, 'What did you do with it?'

James is laid back as he tells us what happened to the car. 'I didn't want anything to do with the car. I keep it in the garage. Never been driven since.'

Jessica and I are overcome with relief when we hear that the car is still in his garage. I do not feel in a hurry to check the car over as we know it is in a safe place. I think about calling Trudy to come sooner to begin her forensic work.

Jessica is trying to contain her joy at knowing that we are close to proving that the stolen car was used to kidnap Daniel. That any evidence could point us to where he may be resting.

I finish my questioning and am keen to recap on James's responses with Jessica back at the trailer. I also want to call Trudy when we leave his house.

WE GO BACK to the police station; we want to follow their protocol for commandeering a vehicle to have it examined. Bob directs us to the appropriate person who completes forms to make it officially legal for us to collect the car.

While we wait for the forms to be completed, I call Trudy and, without saying a word, she says that she is on her way now. She is aiming to get here tonight and book herself into a nice hotel in town. She will let me know when she arrives and settles in.

IT IS NOW after one o'clock and the only thing I can think of is going for lunch. Jessica feels like writing her first article as an opening to getting closer to finding Daniel. As there is nothing much else to do today, Jessica goes into work to prepare her report to go out tomorrow. I tell her that it will make guilty parties nervous if they are still living in town.

I decide to go for a walk and think of any other avenues to investigate.

Also, there is nothing else to do until Trudy arrives. I hope she can find a clue as to where the baseball cap has travelled to and a trace of Daniel in the car. I have ideas of traces floating in my head such as hair, mud, grass, flower, stone or chewing gum. Anything that harbours DNA or a footprint.

WHILE I WALK along South Main Street, I notice the same stares again and recite my conversation with Jessica's dad, Tony. I think his idea of the people knowing why I am here is incorrect. They cannot look me in the eye as I walk past them. I have not seen any black families here since I arrived four days ago.

I quickly move my thoughts to what I have found out so far about the cold case. The three men who saw the boy go into a car does not match up with Alex taking the kid. The stolen black car is a strong contender for the kidnapping. I know that the person who startled Daniel in the lobby is likely a part of the abduction. That one video could solve the case.

THE NEXT PERSON I go to walk past is an elderly woman who must be in her seventies. She stops and gazes at me in surprise.

The elderly woman grabs my arm sincerely and says, 'You are the famous detective. You wrote a few books on finding missing persons. Can I have your autograph? Everyone is talking about you.'

I get flustered not knowing how to react. 'Sure. Where do you want me to sign?'

The elderly lady takes out a book, 'In the cover. Can you write "To Barbara, love Stoane?'

I write inside a copy of my book, 'There you go. How did you know I wrote a book?'

The elderly lady explains, 'Rumour had it that you were in town to investigate an unsolved crime. It does not take long to find out who new visitors are. People looked you up. Realised that you wrote a successful book. If people have been staring at you oddly, it is because you are a bit of a celebrity.'

I do not know how to react. 'I thought being new in town, people were staring at me oddly.'

The elderly woman waves her hand to shrug off my thought. 'No. They don't know how to approach you. They have never been around a famous person before. I think the single women around here want a piece of you. If I was twenty years younger, I would.'

I get embarrassed now. 'I'm sure you're just being kind. I have a wife and two kids. So, I don't need any admirers.'

She giggles and then walks away. I stand there in disbelief at what I have just heard. I see the town differently now and realise why people have behaved oddly around me.

I EVENTUALLY GET BACK to my trailer and pour myself a drink. I have good energy around me and feel like drinking to a good day.

It seems like a Saturday afternoon while I sip my glass of rum. A few minutes later, I hear a knock at the door and assume it is Jessica.

As I go to open the door, I ask her how she finished her article so quickly. However, when I open the door, I see that it is Justine. I cannot hide my surprise and wonder if she is going to complain about something. This is the first time she has come to see me. I assume she is going to do a surprise inspection.

JUSTINE WALKS in uninvited clutching a book under her arm. She is overseeing my trailer like she is checking for faults.

Before I have a chance to make polite conversation, she thrusts the book at me and asks me to sign it for her. I get flustered and write something similar to Barbara, then quickly hand it back to her.

Before I know it, she has me against the wall next to the kitchen and slowly runs her fingers down the front of her top.

Before I have a chance to push her away, I feel her tongue in my mouth. All I can think about is my wife making a surprise entrance. Eventually, I push her off me and, in between deep breaths, explain that I am not a free agent. She is not regretting making a pass at me. She assumes that I have separated from my wife and am using this place as a temporary home.

I reiterate that my relationship is solid and ask her to leave. Before Justine goes, she asks me to sign a copy of my second book. I quickly sign the page and hurry her out.

I THINK I preferred it when I thought people were being covert about the colour of my skin. I do not like having the spotlight on myself. People in New Jersey are uninterested in celebrity and are not easily influenced. I assumed that this town would not be interested in knowing visitors. At least they leave me to get on with my job.

I HAVE a pizza in the freezer and put that in the oven for lunch. While I wait for my lunch, I wonder what Jessica is going to write. I imagine her sat in front of her laptop typing away with her notes and thoughts. I wonder what she will put in the paper and if it will stir any persons involved in the disappearance.

I find myself lost not having anything to do until Trudy gets here. She texted me a while back saying that she was on her way. She should arrive about seven o'clock tonight. She is driving here so she can carry portable equipment to carry out her work. She would not be able to carry them on the plane.

The plan is to have dinner with her, either in her hotel or nearby, to go over what I have found so far with the help of Jessica. Also, it will allow us to catch up properly on our personal lives.

18

AT LAST, A BREAKTHROUGH

It is close to seven o'clock and I have not heard from Jessica. I guess she has gone home now and will see me tomorrow.

I have spent the last few hours mulling over the six people interviewed and the hope of a breakthrough.

I have already had a couple of glasses of rum while waiting for Trudy to arrive in town. It is too early to call Sheila as she will still be working.

Occasionally, I think about the site manager pouncing on me and don't quite believe that really happened. I really do not want to face her anytime soon. At least I have something to talk about with Sheila.

I HEAR my phone make a noise to let me know I have a new text. I know it is Trudy and quickly text back with my address so she can pick me up.

After she collects me, I take her to the same restaurant I went to when I first came here. We do not say much as we want to save it for dinner.

SMOKEY QUE'S is busier since it is a Friday evening. We are still able to find a table for two. Trudy has quickly recognised the way people are staring at us. Later, I explain the reason behind it.

The same woman who served me before comes to show us to a table and take our order. She remembers me and asks how my week has been so far. I smile and say that the people here are friendly and hospitable.

Trudy begins the conversation after settling down, 'How are Sheila and the kids?'

I cannot help picturing them in my mind as she reminds me of them.

'They are all good. Sheila is missing my moans. The kids are now at college. I have been meaning to find out if you have met anyone yet.'

Trudy half laughs and smiles; 'I'm kind of seeing someone. It is very early days. Work is getting in the way; especially you.'

I smile and act like I do not know what she means, 'I just told you about an old case involving a missing child of thirty-eight years. You wanted to come down.'

Trudy laughs at my humour. 'Well, tell me more.'

I tell her what I know so far. 'I reinterviewed three witnesses and three character witnesses. Their stories today are very different to 1982. They all said that they felt the right questions were not asked and felt restricted as to what they could say. On the night of the disappearance of the child, a car was stolen, and a house was burgled. Then there was a truck on fire. The car description given by three of the witnesses is similar to the car that was stolen. I also noticed that the boy was startled at the police station and asked for a video to see who the boy was startled by.'

Trudy goes over what I said; 'You want me to examine the stolen car and you mentioned a baseball cap.'

'Yes. It was found in the accommodation of the man who was jailed for the disappearance.'

Trudy is surprised. 'They arrested a man with no body?'

I react the same way; 'The cap was enough to convict him. It was found in its place, nowhere else.'

Trudy questions my judgement; 'Do you think he is innocent?'

'Yes. His facial expression told he was telling the truth. A senator is convinced he is innocent. The witnesses and a video of the boy are also telling me it wasn't him. When the body is found, that is when we will have our confirmation.'

Trudy is keen to examine both. 'I have the equipment with me to get the forensics done. Is the car at the police station already?'

I have not heard anything new, so I tell her, 'Still waiting for someone to update me. I should hear something tomorrow before lunch. In the meantime, you start on the baseball cap first.'

Our food arrives and we stop talking about work while we enjoy our meal. I feel like the case is moving along now Trudy is here.

DURING OUR DINNER, I find out more about her new potential boyfriend and how they met. I tell her about my brief encounter with fame when an old lady asked for my autograph. Also, I tell her about the site manager thinking I had left my wife. Trudy laughs uncontrollably, finding it highly amusing when I explain how uncomfortable it felt and the fact that I do not go bragging about writing three popular books.

We are the last two here now as it comes to eleven o'clock. The staff are preparing the tables around us for tomorrow and cleaning the floor. We do not realise that this place has already closed as no one asked us to leave.

I PAY the bill and then Trudy drives me back to the trailer park. When we arrive back, I wonder if she wants to see what I have found so far. I ask her and she is half tempted but fights the temptation; she wants to go to bed now and be fresh for tomorrow. She is keen to make headway with her forensic work.

Realistically, I could do with going to bed straight away too.

WHEN I GET INSIDE, I check my phone for messages and see that Jessica sent me a message. I also see a missed call. Her message apologises for not calling me earlier and assumes that I am in bed. She wishes that she had come over to my place instead of going home first. I want to text back, but it is too late, and I do not want to risk waking her up if her phone is not on silent.

I know my wife will be lying in bed also and so I do not want to disturb her sleep. For a moment, I think of having a nightcap, but I know I have already had enough to drink.

SATURDAY DAY 5

I WAKE up naturally to see it is quarter to eight. Jessica is going to be here in fifteen minutes, so I rush out of bed and go straight into the shower. While I wash myself, I get excited about Trudy finding clues to what happened to Daniel from his cap and the hope of finding out that the stolen car was involved in his disappearance. This could break the case wide open.

I come out of the shower and see the time is close to seven fifty-five. I still have five minutes before Jessica arrives.

I hear my phone ping and assume it is Trudy. I check my phone while trying to put my shirt on at the same time. She is texting to say that she is on her way and will be here in five minutes. As I finish reading the text, Jessica arrives and knocks on the door.

I have managed to get myself fully dressed before she arrived. I shout out for Jessica to let herself in.

Jessica apologises for last night. 'I didn't get home until after eight and by the time I finished making myself relaxed, I felt it was too late to call.'

I let her know that it is okay. 'No problem. I know you were writing up your article. When does it come out?'

Jessica is relieved that she didn't upset me, 'Phew, I was worried that you were expecting me. So, what did you get up to last night? Anything exciting?'

I can only think about being pounced on, so I tell her, 'Justine, the site manager, made a pass at me.'

Jessica's jaw drops, 'You are kidding. How did that happen?'

I awkwardly act out where it happened. 'I was here, and she came right at me and made a pass. She literally rammed her tongue down my throat. I felt like my privacy was invaded. She thought I'd left my wife.'

JESSICA CANNOT STOP LAUGHING and wished she had come over now to see it. Briefly, she wonders what Justine felt kissing him. Her feelings for him are still getting stronger and she does not know how to suppress them.

She wants the investigation to conclude sooner so she can spend time alone to allow herself to move on from him.

ONCE JESSICA COMPOSES HERSELF, she asks if Trudy has arrived here yet. I let her know that I went out for dinner with her, and we caught up on our daily lives.

Before I can tell Jessica, that Trudy is coming over, she appears at the trailer. I introduce them to each other briefly before the three of us head to the police station. I bring with us the baseball cap, still in the original evidence bag. We go in Trudy's car as her car is an SUV and has all her equipment inside. The two of them sit in the front and blank me like I am not there.

DURING OUR JOURNEY THERE, Jessica and Trudy get to know each other properly.

Trudy begins the conversation; 'So, what's it like working with Cold?'

Jessica is hesitant as she turns to me, 'He is okay. Makes me drive around everywhere like I am his chauffeur.'

I jump in, 'My car got vandalised. Tyres are slashed.'

Trudy is amused. 'Sure you didn't do it yourself to get out of it?'

Jessica tries not to chortle. 'How do you know each other?'

Trudy tells her the story; 'Well, I was asked to attend a crime scene and I happened to be on a date. He thought I was a reporter and pushed me behind the crime scene tape. I had to go all the way home to get my ID badge.'

I quickly explain myself; 'I had never met you before. You could have been a fraudster.'

Trudy sucks her teeth; 'I had my kit on me.'

Jessica laughs at our banter. 'That is a great story. What was he like as a cop?'

'He was good. He spotted things that no one else did. He had an eye for detail. So, I'm not surprised why he was asked to solve this case. There isn't a case he hasn't solved. If it wasn't for his temper...'

I interrupt, 'She doesn't need to know that.'

Trudy goes quiet and realises that she almost overstepped the mark. 'Well, that is all I have to say about how we get on.'

We arrive outside the police station and Trudy decides to get her equipment and carry it inside. Jessica and I help her.

I have butterflies in my stomach as we are going to find out where Daniel made his last journey.

Bob has already allocated a room downstairs in the basement of the station that is used for the storage of old furniture.

Trudy has a portable bench to work on and sets up her equipment. She has the latest data sample software with hundreds of thousands of samples pre-stored.

Once she is fully set up, I give her the unopened bag containing the cap and she begins to check for samples on the fabric.

The man who helped me to organise for the car to be collected comes to see me. He has good news that the car has been collected and is in the compound for inspection. Jessica and I are excited that Trudy can also use her forensic skills on that.

Trudy pauses as she goes to open the evidence bag. 'What do you want me to do first?'

I mull the decision over in my head, then say, 'I think the car first. Yes, the car.'

Trudy is not bothered which one she begins examining.

The man shows us to the back of the police station to the compound for vehicles held as evidence. Trudy takes her metal box that holds the utensils for collecting samples and blue surgical gloves so as not to contaminate evidence.

The car has a film of dust over the body, and you can see it has not been touched in years. The bodywork appears to be intact. There is no rust along the chassis, and it is like it has never been driven.

Trudy takes the lead by taking the car keys that the man is dangling in front of us. She gently unlocks the car and the door clunks open. She gingerly opens the s side door as if the car is fragile.

She observes what is inside the car without touching anything. Jessica and I keep at a distance and wait for her to finish what she is doing. The man has already left us to it having no interest in our examination.

A few moments later, she walks past us. 'I need gloves, tweezers and a magnifying glass. There are lots of samples to collect. I think we have a breakthrough. There is chewing gum, grass and dirt and that is just the footwell.'

Jessica tugs Trudy's arm and says, 'But that could be the owner of the car.'

Trudy thinks differently. 'How many times do you throw your food on the floor in your own car?'

I like the way she thinks. 'Exactly. Mark's dad, James, told us that he couldn't get rid of it and asked him to use it. If you love your car that much, you wouldn't so much as leave a scuff mark.'

Jessica now understands as she considers how she treats her car. 'How will the chewing gum help with the case?'

Trudy explains what she will do with the sample; 'There will be saliva inside the gum. I extract that and analyse the DNA, hoping that the person who chewed this is on the database for some other crime.'

Jessica is curious and asks, 'How do you know it will be likely that they will be on the system?'

I explain the theory behind it. 'Whoever harmed the kid is likely to be a repeat offender. If you get away with it the first time, you don't see it as a one-time thing.'

I take a couple of small evidence bags and a pair of disposable blue gloves from Trudy's metal case.

I open the trunk and use the flats of my fingers to feel for any loose particles. I find soil, which you would normally find in a car being transferred from boots and shoes. Even so, I still bag the sample in case it could be helpful. Nothing obvious stands out and so I randomly collect anything loose and foreign to the car.

There are no bloodstains to take samples of that would relate to the boy.

I hear Trudy in the back of the car now, foraging for further samples of evidence. When I am finished with the trunk, I get into the driver's side and check under the seat. I see a cigarette butt and frantically reach in my pocket for another evidence bag to nimbly extract it and place it inside the bag. I feel a moment of joy before scanning for more potential evidence.

Almost an hour later, Trudy and I have collected a dozen samples in readiness for testing. This is great news.

19

A LEAD

From the samples that Trudy and I have collected, the chewing gum is the obvious choice for testing first.

One of the pieces of equipment she has brought in from her car is a QIAamp DNA Micro Kit. It will be used to extract any saliva held for the past thirty-nine years.

Trudy says that it will take her a couple of hours to analyse the sample. She will get all the samples tested today. She is thinking that it will take her till late tonight to gather the results.

To fill the day while we are waiting, Jessica decides to write another article on what we have achieved today.

I keep Trudy company providing coffee and going to the nearby grocery store for snacks. While I am observing her work, I get a phone call and do not recognise the number. I wait for my cell phone to ring out and see if a message is left.

A text comes through from the same number asking how the case is going. I realise it is Senator Charleston. I tell Trudy I have to make a phone call and leave the room to call him back.

I STAND in the corridor just outside the room and call the senator back.

Senator Charleston answers, 'Hello, how is it going down there?'

I choose not to tell him of my progress, so simply tell him, 'It is going okay.'

Senator Charleston tries to push for details; 'You've been there five days now. You must have something.'

I decide to give him something that is nothing. 'We have found some potential new evidence that we are testing out. Everyone is saying what they originally said thirty-eight years ago.'

Senator Charleston goes quiet, but I can hear him breathing sporadically. 'There is something you need to know.'

I wonder what is worrying him, so I ask, 'What's wrong? Tell me.'

Senator Charleston is panicking. 'I heard that the President is issuing some consents now that he is on his way out.'

I find myself getting impatient now. 'Spit it out. I need to be somewhere now.'

Senator Charleston finally comes out with it. 'He has signed the Alex Jefferson death sentence to take place in three days.'

I am not sure if I heard him correctly, so I insist, 'Say that again.'

Senator Charleston says what I hope he did not. 'Alex is going to face the death sentence in three days' time. If you have anything, now would be a good time.'

I go quiet and assess where we are and anticipate how much further we need to be. 'We are analysing some samples. There has been no breakthrough with the case yet. If there is something to prove his innocence, I will find it. What time will they put him to sleep?'

Senator Charleston sounds scared when he says, 'It is normally late morning, around eleven o'clock. That gives you just under thirty-six hours.'

I feel the pressure is on now, so I tell him, 'I gotta go. Will let you know when I find the killer. Just keep me informed of any changes to his appointment with death.'

The senator reassures me that he will, and I hang up. I stand still allowing the news to sink in. I work backwards to pre-empt what Trudy and I will have to do to pull off a miracle.

I GO BACK inside the room in a daze then I walk up to Trudy to see where she is with testing the gum.

Trudy hears me and turns round. 'What is it? You look as if you have seen a ghost.'

I only catch the last bit of her sentence. 'I just might if we do not find the real killer.'

Trudy is puzzled; 'What's going on?'

'Alex Jefferson is going to be put to death in three days' time. Eleven o'clock in the morning.'

Trudy sees the gravity of the situation. 'Do you believe he is innocent?'

I think about the time frame; 'We have to get all these samples tested today and then see where it leads us.'

Trudy holds my wrist and says, 'I didn't ask you about the evidence leading us to the truth. Do you think Alex is innocent?'

I watch her staring into my eyes for an answer. 'Yes. My gut tells me he is innocent. Please tell me you can pull off a miracle.'

Trudy lets go of my wrist. 'Well, let's use the evidence to prove that someone else did it. He only has us to stop him from frying in the chair or a lethal chemical injection.'

She gives me hope that we will get to the bottom of what happened and who framed him.

IT IS A LONG DAY, and by eight o'clock, Trudy has finished examining all the samples. Interestingly, Trudy begins with the baseball cap instead of the chewing gum.

She uses her laptop to show the results. 'The cap has only one type of blood and you have to assume it is the boy's. But the strand of hair I found does not match the blood DNA. So, we have two people who touched this cap. We need to go on CODIS to see if anyone has their DNA in the system.'

I ask her about the other samples; 'What about the chewing gum? Does that match the blood or the hair?'

'No. The gum shows a third DNA which means that there were two or three people in the car. Now, there is something else that is going to blow your mind.'

I think back to what Mark's dad said and tell Trudy, 'James did say his son saw three people stealing the car. Even if one of the DNA samples belongs to the boy, there is a third person unaccounted for. We find the other two, we find the third person. Alex's DNA will be on the database from when he was convicted. So, if none of the three pops him up, we have our proof he is innocent. What was the other thing that is going to blow my mind?'

Trudy gets excited as she tells me, 'I noticed that there were traces of metal on the cap. Wasn't sure what it meant. Figured that he had been to an abandoned factory. The computer came up with a car. Thought I would take a sample from the car. Chip some off from under the car chassis. You know what I found?'

I know where she is going, 'Both the metal on the cap and the car match.'

Trudy nods her head, 'You got it. How did you come up with the idea that this car was involved in the kidnap?'

I tell her about the car being in a report in the same newspaper as the story of the boy's disappearance. 'I had a hunch. Three men were parked opposite the police station and saw the boy go in a car with a description close to the stolen car. But they were too stoned to be accurate. So, now we have concrete evidence that the car was used to kidnap the boy, what do we know about the dirt and grass I found in the trunk of the car?'

Trudy smiles as she goes to read the results. 'Now, I ran the soil and grass against the database for plants and dirt. Did you know that there are hundreds of different kinds of grass and mud?'

'I do now. Tell me that you found something.'

Trudy goes into a zone; 'I cross-referenced the land with the samples we have. Did you know that Marion has different soil compositions in each forest section? And mixed with the grass was a stem of a flower. Helleborus orientalis, also known as the Lenten Rose. It is only found in one place. I think God is on our side today.'

I have a smile all of a sudden. 'Please tell me you have co-ordinates to this particular part of the woods?'

Trudy gives me the biggest grin, 'You betcha. There is a road that can lead us to the entrance of the forest. The road name is Cove Forest Road. I think we now know what we are going to do tomorrow.'

Without thinking, I give Trudy a huge hug and a sigh of relief that we are finally getting somewhere.

IT IS NOW after nine o'clock and we decide to finish for the night. I help Trudy to pack her equipment up, but we will keep it here. She has a feeling that there will be more testing to be done after tomorrow.

Trudy drives me back to my trailer park and I ask if she wants to come in briefly. She wants to have an early night and be fresh for tomorrow. I understand what she means and get out of the car.

Justine appears and taps on the driver's side window. We both jump and realise it is the site manager.

I walk around the front of the car and ask what she is doing out here so late. She thought I had brought a woman home with me. Thinking we were an item, she almost read me the riot act for bringing a woman back to the trailer.

I wonder if she remembers pouncing on me yesterday and the 'Pot calling the kettle black' springs to mind.

Trudy rolls the window down and laughs at her accusation and reassures her that we are friends. She slowly reverses out of the park.

JUSTINE ASKS if I want company and I quickly say that I am going to bed alone. I pretend to yawn to emphasise the alone part.

I find she has some cheek accusing me of bringing a woman back when she wants to come into my trailer at this time of night.

I CLOSE the door behind me and decide to have one glass of rum before changing into my pyjamas and going to bed.

20

FROZEN EVIDENCE

Sunday Day 6

IT IS JUST after eight o'clock and Jessica is arriving now. She knocks on the door as per usual and I shout for her to come in.

Jessica asks how last night went. 'Did you manage to get all the samples analysed? I thought I would hear from you last night.'

'Trudy tested all the examples. We need to cross-match the three DNAs from the baseball cap and chewing gum. She found that the grass I found in the trunk included a stem from a flower. There is only one place it can be found in the area. That is where we are going today. The only way to get there is via Cove Forest Road. Did you manage to get the second article finished in time for today's print?'

Jessica is wondering when we finished testing. 'Yeah. I was finished by five o'clock again. I was hoping you would text me when you were finished. When do you want to head out to Cove Forest Road? I'm ready to go now.'

I remember that Trudy is coming over, so I tell her, 'We have to wait for Trudy. She should be here anytime soon. She will drive us there.'

Through the window, I see Trudy driving up. I have a strange feeling that today will be a sad day. It is the gut feeling that I get whenever a case is close to completing.

WE DO NOT WASTE time getting into her car and using Jessica's direction to travel to the area that grows the Lenten Rose.

It does not take long before we reach the outskirts of town and drive through the woodlands along a black tarmac road.

It reminds me of when I drove into town at night-time, driving through a similar forest along a single road.

When we reach the junction with Cove Forest Road, Jessica asks Trudy to slow down and prepare for a sharp turn to the left.

As we drive into the road, the trees block out the sunlight and the car's auto lights come on. I think we are here, but Jessica says that it is another few yards before we reach the edge of the forest.

When we reach the dead-end where the road meets the forest, Trudy turns the engine off. We all climb out of the car and make our way into an open area in front of the woodland.

I feel that we are beginning to reach the end of our quest to find the remains of Daniel Harris. It is not a good feeling; it's like you are about to face death. If we were hunting for treasure, I would be feeling excited about coming close to finding the treasure chest. But when searching for a missing person, you never want to find them as you know it is never a nice ending. I do not convey my feelings to Trudy or Jessica as I do not want to make it feel real with my thoughts out in the open.

As we walk into the open area before the tree trunks begin, I have a desire to protect Jessica's eyes from the harsh reality of finding human remains. I ask Jessica to stay behind Trudy so she does not see something that will haunt her for the rest of her life.

Trudy has a sense she will find fresh evidence here, so she warns me, 'Stoane, if you see anything, don't touch it. Just give me a holler and I will see if it is worth bagging.'

Jessica is beginning to feel worried. 'I think this place is eerie. Do you two have the same feeling?'

I make light of the mood by saying, 'It is like going for a hike. It only feels eerie because no one is around, and we have low light here. Nothing is going to happen to us.'

Trudy passes comment as well; 'I have been on a lot of excursions following a lead or a hunch. I have never once been startled. It is all in the mind.'

Jessica seems to be more relaxed now.

. . .

THE OPEN AREA has thick lush green grass where it has not been disturbed. The woods begin about twenty feet away. I lead the way into the woods having an idea what we should find.

There is an obvious dirt track that has been created by vehicles. For some reason, the ground has not recovered which must be from the lack of sunlight and warmth.

Trudy focuses on the leaves that we found small specks of in the car. We hope that this is the first and last place we will have to visit. Jessica and I watch her do her work.

I notice that Jessica is intrigued by how Trudy uses her forensic experience. She watches her with a small torch shining on the foliage near our legs. Trudy has concentration on her face as if she is studying an insect.

I realise how far we have walked along the track and see that the makeshift road is not coming to an end anytime soon. I suggest we go back to the SUV and drive through here. They agree and Trudy offers to get the car.

While we wait, I make small talk; 'Did you envisage us going on a field trip into the woods?'

Jessica is a little fidgety, but replies, 'Kind of. If we're going to find Daniel, it wouldn't be in a café, right?'

I chortle at her comment; 'No. Whatever happens today, it is not as bad what people might think.'

Jessica shows a confused expression when she asks, 'How do you mean?'

I am frank with her; 'I think this place will give us a clue to where he is. If we find him, I don't want you to be scared or alarmed. He is at peace. His soul is no longer here.'

Jessica is realising that we are actually searching for the body now. 'I thought we were finding the men who took him.'

I give a gentle smile as I say, 'The whole reason for this expedition and Trudy being here is to find Daniel first. Then he will lead us to the perpetrators. That is how it works. The victim leads us to the person or persons who did it.'

We hear Trudy driving towards us and see the headlights.

WHEN SHE CATCHES up with us, I take the driver's side and have Jessica sit in the back. I cautiously drive along the trail feeling for divots and looking out for stray branches overhanging our path. I can hear the wheels breaking twigs.

You cannot see an ending to this path, and it feels eerie where the thick leafy branches block any daylight.

After about ten minutes, we eventually come to an open area and see a cabin.

. . .

It is a typical dark brown wooden structure that appears abandoned. Long beige grass, a foot tall, creates a perimeter around the dilapidated structure. The roof is collapsing in the middle and there is a crooked chimney on the side.

There are single framed windows on either side of the front door. You cannot see inside as it is too dark. My senses are heightened as to what this place could hold.

Trudy shows concern on her face as she has been to many scenes like this. Jessica is curious with an innocent expression, and I remind her to stay behind us.

There is a large field that goes around the side of the cabin and is a couple of acres at the back. You can see that no one lives here, and it has been abandoned for years.

Trudy focuses on the plants surrounding us and I can guess she is searching for the Lenten Rose I found in the trunk of the stolen car. It is not long before she finds a patch growing among the grass. She is looking for a particular leaf. It is a light green leaf and looks a tiny bit like cannabis. It does not naturally grow everywhere and hence why we will know when we find the right location.

Jessica makes notes of what we have discovered while we feel out the place. I am half expecting to find a shallow grave, or the boy's remains lying on top of the soil among the grass. I begin to have flashes of what his body could be like after thirty-eight years.

Trudy and I are used to seeing human remains, but I know Jessica would freak out. I ask her to stay by the car while we carry out a recce.

We spread out and cover about an acre within a radius of the cabin. It is an open area where you can see miles of rolling hills and mountains in the backdrop.

It is not long before I notice a certain kind of plant. I crouch down to make a better assessment. I can see this field used to be used to grow cannabis.

The ground has been undisturbed for months if not years. Trudy walks over and she concludes the same.

Trudy has not found any signs of human burial or remains. She confirms that she found patches of the plant found in the stolen car. We both agree that this is the place. We quickly come to the conclusion that the boy must have seen something that caused his disappearance.

Trudy wants to go inside to see what we can find. I think we have reached the end of the road to finding Daniel. I stop Trudy from walking ahead of us and make sure they are both behind me.

The door is locked, which I already expected, and I consider smashing one of the windows to get inside. Instead, I have a try at dislodging the door as it is old and decaying. I allow room to take a straight kick to the door lock. After the third attempt, the door finally caves in with a piece of the right side of the doorframe splitting.

I ASK Trudy and Jessica to wait here while I go in first. I do not want them to see any unexpected frightening scenes.

Inside is dark as barely any light comes in. There is an old damp smell in the air. There is no sign of habitation.

There are cobwebs in the corners of the ceiling and the wooden floor is dusty but with no disturbance. The floorboards creak occasionally.

The immediate room is the living area with a fireplace that has some cobwebs around the outside. I walk up to double-check if it has been used recently. I put my hand out above the black burnt-out logs. It is stone cold.

I hear a creaking noise and quickly turn round to see if it is the women. They freeze and I go to where I heard the noise.

THERE ARE two bedrooms opposite the fireplace, and I go into the left room where I think the noise came from.

I raise my right arm expecting to take a swing at someone. The door is wide open, and I peer inside, stretching my neck. I cannot see anything. I can see the bed is stripped of any bedding and the room is empty. I go inside the second bedroom, and it appears to be the same.

I NOW DECIDE to walk to the back room, which I assume is the kitchen, and see a door to the back. I wave to the women to come inside.

There are cobwebs on the work surface as well as dust. An old aged stainless-steel kettle sits on the slightly rusty stove. Jessica is reluctant but follows behind Trudy. I motion to them to still keep a distance of a couple of feet behind me.

The kitchen units are old and dated with brown cupboards and the stove is off-white in colour. I open a couple of cupboards to see if I can find any provisions with a sell-by date to work out when this place last had occupants. All the cupboards are bare; not even dinner plates or cutlery.

I see a door that I assume leads out to the back. When I open the door, I see that it is a small utility corridor leading to the back door.

I SEE a freezer unit that you use for storing oversized meat that cannot go in a normal upright freezer. My instinct tells me to get the women to step away and not to turn around until I say it is okay.

I take a deep breath, close my eyes and turn away as I pull the door up to open the freezer.

21

FOLLOW THE CLUE

After I open the freezer door, I gradually turn around to see inside. As I do, Trudy shrieks, which makes me jump and almost give me a heart attack. I hush her when she asks me if we have found what we came here for.

I turn my head to see what is inside, and, to my horror, we finally find Daniel Harris.

MY GUT FEELING turned out to be true. His last journey ended up inside a six-by-three-foot chest freezer.

I do not ask either of them to come closer. The remains have been preserved by the lack of air inside the unit. It still distresses me as my mind comes to terms with what my eyes can see. I imagine if it had been one of my children who had succumbed to this.

Trudy asks me what I can see, and I have to compose myself before I can say anything as I try to block out the image.

I take Jessica outside as Trudy goes to see for herself. She can see by my face that it is bad but nothing she has not seen before. She has a sombre expression as she knows what she will find.

WHEN I TAKE Jessica outside to the back of the cabin, she is a white as a sheet as she already knows what I am about to say.

I hold her hands firmly as I try to prepare her; 'We found him. His family can finally find peace, not that they will be comforted.'

Jessica slowly comes round to the realisation that the mystery of the disappearance is over. 'Could you see if he suffered?'

I have an idea from my experience of homicides, so I can say, 'No. Not like that. But I think he only suffered briefly. He would not have known his fate when he went in that car. Now, I believe he will lead us to his killer stroke killers. I can tell he wanted to be a detective when he was growing up. I have a hunch he has helped to point us in the right direction.'

Jessica understands and leaves me to make some important phone calls.

TRUDY CAN SEE ONLY a segment of Daniel Harris's face. She can build the rest of his face in her mind and can see how peaceful he is. This is not her first exposure to a dissembled body but not as young as him.

She knows that his remains will have to be taken back to the police department and analysed there. For now, she considers what evidence she can get from under his fingernails.

I HAVE the sheriff on the phone. 'Yeah. How soon can you come out here to tape off this place and have the coroner out here?'

Sheriff Bob is keen to get things moving like yesterday, so he says, 'The coroner will be out there in five minutes. I will have two cop cars out there to quickly cordon off the crime scene. And thanks.'

I sigh and say, 'My pleasure. I wish it could be under nicer circumstances like a fall or a trip down an embankment. Not the way he went.'

Sheriff Bob sounds emotional; 'I want to find the bastards who did this. You don't carry a badge anymore?'

I know what he is suggesting. 'I retired. I have a senator backing me financially.'

Sheriff Bob goes quiet, then says, 'I promise, whatever happens, I'll have your back.'

I eventually get off the phone with him and check to see that Jessica is okay. For a second, I think about the autopsy and my wife. It will make sense to ask my wife to come down here and lend her assistance.

I give her a call hoping she will pick up now. 'Hi, I have a favour to ask.'

Sheila knows why I have called her. 'You found the body. That poor child. Have the parents been informed yet?'

'I have not said anything yet, but I want to hold off on telling his parents. I don't want the killer to know that we have found the body. That means not leaking it to the press. That could help stop the person or persons from running away.'

IT IS NOW close to two o'clock and police officers are already here taping off the cabin. The boy's body has been carried out to the coroner's car.

Sheriff Bob is observing the area in dismay, wondering why his people did not think to come out here to find him.

Jessica, Trudy and I are huddled together by the car watching the police finish cordoning off the area. Sheriff Bob finally walks over to us.

SHERIFF BOB WANTS to talk to me privately, so he says, 'Excuse us, ladies. I want to talk to Stoane alone.'

Trudy understands and says, 'Come on, Jessica, we will wait in the car.'

I follow him away from the car and prying ears. 'What's up?'

Sheriff Bob wants to continue the conversation we had on the phone. 'I want the men responsible for his death. There is no way that Alex could have done this and not have a lot more blood on that cap. We did not find any bloody clothing at his place at the time. No other piece of evidence was there.'

I am shocked to hear him say this. 'So, what has changed your tune?'

Sheriff Bob gives a sigh, then says, 'The body was chopped up. That takes a lot of time. There was no saw found in his place. The weapon is still at large. The body was left in a freezer unit in a cabin that has never been lived in. No one knew that this place existed until now. This area was never searched. He did not own a car. I assume the mud on the car will match up with the dirt track.'

I agree with him; 'You're not a sleepy cop after all. What do you have in mind?'

Sheriff Bob ignores my question. 'I assume you spotted the remains of cannabis growing out the back. No sign of dwelling here. No homeless persons. That field was not exactly a home vegetable patch. Did you notice a couple of acid bottles and a metal drum around the back?'

I hadn't noticed but put forward my opinion of what was planned; 'He was going to be dissolved beyond existence. Something spooked them. Hide the body in the freezer to be disposed of later. You got something else that springs to mind?'

Sheriff Bob reads my mind; 'The place was cleaned from top to bottom. No trace of fingerprints or someone ever being here. The beds were stripped. I wasn't born in the Stone Age to know that this is bigger than a kid going missing. A kid going missing is being found in a river, hedge or buried, not prepared for being dissolved in acid. Alex was heading to university. We questioned the university to be told he had a place there.'

I think we are definitely on the same wavelength. 'Drugs being grown and distributed across town and maybe sold in other nearby towns. What made you see this so soon? You have only been here two minutes.'

Sheriff Bob has an eye for detail. 'Like I said, I was not born in the Stone Age. I have seen a lot over the years and kept my ear to the ground. There is a particular acid that only burns clean through human tissue. You can't buy that here. That would have to be bought from a large depot. Again, Alex wouldn't have a clue where to go for that. His profile type would just ditch a body where no one could find it. A paedophile would not have the brain cells to come up with an idea like this. You and Trudy found him in six days. What can you do in another six days?'

I am not sure what he wants me to do, so I say, 'I am assuming that there will be evidence on the remains, like skin, hair or maybe blood. Like you said, the killer panicked. He planned on getting rid of the evidence. Why get rid of any evidence of the remains when the acid would do that? So, we could find the killer in a matter of days. What is your stress?'

Sheriff Bob makes sure no one can hear us. 'I don't just want these people found. I read your file. You are a bit of a dark horse. I know you got fired. But you were a hell of a cop.'

I see where he is coming from and assure him, 'I vowed never to be that person again.'

Sheriff Bob's eyes are begging me to be that person one more time. 'I have ways of making people talk, if that is what you mean. I will make sure they get justice the legal way.'

Sheriff Bob oversteps the line by saying, 'What if he was black? This was in the south.'

I step away from him and insist, 'This is not about skin colour. I was asked by the senator to look into the case. I am doing that. The boy could have been Indian. It would not change my stance. Now, I promise I will find the men who did this.'

I walk away before I say something I will regret.

22

PROFILE

When I get into the car, Trudy asks me what we talked about. I do not mention what Sheriff Bob asked me to do but that he wants us to find the boy's killers.

Trudy slowly nods her head in agreement.

SHEILA IS in their bedroom collecting clothes for a few days. She wants to spend time with her husband as well as help with the cause of death.

She is going to drive all the way to Marion in her Land Rover. It will take her almost ten hours to reach there. She plans on leaving before three o'clock and arriving there before midnight.

She decides to dress in a nice way to surprise him. She takes a small suit-case to place her day-to-day clothes in. Her work scrubs are packed in a shop-ping bag to avoid cross-contamination and getting her nice clothes dirty.

She calls Josh and William to let them know that she is going to see their father. She also checks that they have their own key to get into the house. She then calls her husband to let him know that she is on her way now and what her estimated time of arrival is.

WE ARE at the police station now and the coroner has taken the remains to the basement. Two men manage to wheel the mortuary trolley into the lift. They are surprised to see the room is not laid out in the manner of a formal autopsy. They leave the trolley with us.

Jessica and I see some old desks and place them in the middle of the room lengthways. We then slide the body bag over onto the desks.

Trudy asks when Sheila will be here to examine the remains to give us a cause of death. I tell her that she texted me and the message said that she would be here late tonight. She thinks it will be a hindrance if she begins taking samples from the body now. I agree with her and say that another day will not make a difference.

There is nothing else we can do now and decide to go back to my place and relax.

I tell Jessica that she cannot write up her third article on the discovery of the body. I explain to her that if she does, it will hit the local news and spook the killer.

The only people who know of this are Sheriff Bob, Trudy and Jessica. The police officers were not involved in the knowledge of the contents of the bag.

Before we leave, I go to see the sheriff.

SHERIFF BOB IS in his office staring at his laptop, signing off reports. I close the door behind me to shut out any prying colleagues. I ask what he told the police officers on the scene. He reassures me that all they know is it is a homeless man and a suspicious death. He also told them that they are not to mention the area as it could be an old drug-harvesting field. I feel that they could still tell someone, but the sheriff reassures me that he threatened their jobs if they mention the site to anyone. That is good enough for me.

Before I walk out, he asks me what my next step is. I tell him that my wife will be carrying out an autopsy tomorrow to find out how he died. Then Trudy will take samples to test for DNA and maybe some fingerprints. I make clear that I will do everything above board, and they will face the full brunt of the law.

I ask him about Alex's potential release with the new theory, but as I guessed, evidence is needed for someone else to be the suspect. But he is keen to find the culprit as he believes in justice as much as me.

Sheriff Bob has already built up a picture of who the person could be without waiting for the autopsy. He believes it is drug-related and the kid, being so young, had no idea of the risk.

I think about the boy's reaction when he left the police station knowing that someone working here at the time must have been involved. I choose not to mention my theory as I want to keep it close to my chest for now.

Now I have spoken to him about the police officers keeping quiet, I head back to my trailer with Jessica and Trudy.

When we get back to my trailer, they are happy to stay for a while to discuss today's events. We sit at the table in the kitchen area having coffee.

I mention to Trudy and Jessica about Sheriff Bob's theory and agreeing with him about Daniel stumbling upon a cannabis field. This would also give the reason why his remains are the way they are due to a plan to dissolve his body.

Jessica is managing to cope with being told how Daniel's body was left. She stays focused, though, by behaving as a reporter. She continues to take notes for her next article, which she will write when I give her the go-ahead.

Trudy does not think that Sheriff Bob's theory is far-fetched. 'The way the body had been discarded, it fits the modus operandi of a drug dealer making a witness disappear. Sorry. I mean M.O.'

I knew what she meant. 'I'm sure Jessica knew what M. O. was short for. Bob also saw bottles of acid and an oil drum out back.'

Jessica wonders how today's find will help us to catch the killer, so she asks us, 'What are you two hoping to use to solve the murder?'

'My wife will help us to determine what was used to maim the child. Trudy will then find any fibre, foreign skin and anything else on the remains. The boy must have clawed his killer or maybe bitten him.'

Trudy elaborates; 'I will make a thorough examination of anything in his hair, fingernails, marks on his skin. Use that to identify his attacker.'

Jessica finishes taking notes on what we have discussed as our next step.

It is close to eleven o'clock now and I want to take time tidying up the trailer before my wife arrives tonight. We naturally come to a close and they leave at the same time.

After they have gone, I call my wife to see how much longer she will be.

Sheila finishes talking to her husband and is still expecting to reach Marion by midnight. She made a couple of stops to use the restroom and buy provisions.

After another twenty minutes of driving, she decides to stop at a gas station that she has noticed. As Sheila pulls up, she notices from the Sat Nav that she has only ten minutes of her journey left.

She gets out of her car and walks inside the shop to buy a bottle of water and stretch her legs. She sees an old man behind the counter and acknowledges him. When she approaches the counter, the old man remembers seeing Stoane and wonders if she is with him.

The old man rubs his bearded chin and asks, 'You wouldn't happen to be visiting a black chap who wears a raincoat?'

Sheila smiles. 'What gave it away?'

The old man is blunt; 'We don't get many black folks around these parts.'

Sheila finds him amusing. 'Well, I'm his wife.'

'I figured. I saw he had a wedding ring on. How is he getting on with the case of the missing boy?'

Sheila is taken aback. 'How did you know that he was in town for that?'

The old man scratches his beard. 'Rumour travels. He's been here six days now. I figure he is good at his job.'

Sheila takes her change and the bottle and says, 'He does the best he can.'

The old man wishes her well and watches her leave.

As Sheila walks towards her car, she catches her stocking on something and tears it. There is a long tear along her thigh. She is annoyed but cannot do anything about it.

JUSTINE BROWN, the site manager, is in her reception cabin flicking through a magazine out of boredom. She is disappointed not to have found an excuse to lecture a patron.

As she tries to find a good gossip column in the entertainment magazine, she hears a car driving onto the site. She wonders who it could be as everyone is in and there are no vacant trailers.

She sees a black Land Rover drive past the window and is instantly curious to know who it could be. She waits a moment before peeking outside the door without being seen. She sees a black woman come out of the car that is parked outside Stoane's trailer.

The woman's ankle-length black coat blows as she strides over to one of the trailers. Justine is open-mouthed when she catches a glimpse of her torn black stocking.

Justine is devasted to see that Stoane has arranged for a lady of the night to come to his trailer, considering she offered herself to him the other day and he turned her down saying that he is happily married. Now, she sees that he has chosen to pay for a woman rather than have a sophisticated lady such as herself.

With the thought of the woman coming here to satisfy a man's whim, Justine storms towards the trailer. She has thoughts going through her mind of promiscuous sexual activities. The more she overthinks, the angrier she gets as she goes to bang on the door.

She waits for a response for a few seconds before she takes out her master keys. Eventually, she finds the key to the trailer and barges inside.

When she opens the door, Justine is shocked to see Stoane and the woman in the kitchen with the woman lying on the small table with Stoane on top.

AS I AM MAKING love to Sheila unconventionally on the round kitchen table, we hear the door barge open. I turn my head to see who is interrupting our throes of passion.

I cannot believe it is Justine and we both try to cover ourselves up in embarrassment, our privacy invaded.

Sheila is flabbergasted. 'Who is she? How do you know each other?'

I cannot believe this is happening and yell, 'Justine! What the heck are you doing here? This is my wife, Sheila. She came down to help me out on the case.'

Justine is flustered and stutters, 'I'm... so sorry. I thought you were a prostitute. I thought you didn't mean the part about being happily married still. You know people aren't allowed to come in at this hour.'

I bark at her, 'She is my wife. I pay rent here. We have not seen each other in almost a week.'

Justine is trying not to laugh. 'Really sorry. I will take off a day's rent because of the inconvenience.'

I cannot believe the cheek of her. 'How about half the week? Look how distraught my wife is.'

Justine is surprised at my anger and says, 'Of course. I will only charge you for four nights this week.'

I watch her almost trip over her feet, rushing out of the trailer.

JUSTINE SLAMS the door behind her and blushes while trying not to laugh at what just happened. She quietly giggles to herself as she walks back to her office.

AFTER HEARING JUSTINE BURST IN, my appetite has suddenly gone. I cannot get back into the mood. Sheila thinks the same and suggests having a shower and then going to bed.

She realises how tacky the place is and wonders why I could not have found a nicer place to stay.

23

A BREAK IN THE CASE

Monday Day 7

I WAKE up forgetting that Sheila is here lying next to me. For a second, I think about making love to her before Jessica and Trudy arrive, but the thought of being caught again as I attempt to have intimacy stops me. I can imagine Jessica happily walking in.

Sheila wants me to make us breakfast before we head to the police station to autopsy the body.

WE HAVE black coffee with our bacon, eggs and toast. I get Sheila up to date with how far we have moved the cold case along. For obvious reasons, we did not have time to discuss it last night.

I think about what I have told her already. 'Since I last told you about linking the stolen car to the disappearance of the boy, we have found some evidential samples. That led us out into the woods, where we finally found Daniel Harris's body. We have him at the police station and we are crossing our fingers that we can find DNA leading to the killer.'

Sheila is fascinated by the case and adds, 'And, you want me to use my skills to find out how he died and disprove how the current suspect in jail could not have done it.'

I smile at her comment. 'Well, I forgot to mention that the sheriff came to his own conclusion. He noticed some acid bottles and a drum. He seems to think that Daniel may have stumbled on a crop of cannabis. By the way his body was left.'

Sheila does not find his theory far-fetched and agrees, 'I can see that. I have seen everything on my watch. When are we going in?'

I remind her about the girls. 'Trudy and Jessica are coming round here and then we are going in one car.'

'Ah, I forgot. When did you say they come over?'

I wash down my last piece of breakfast with my coffee and say, 'Eight. They are punctual.'

Sheila checks the time on her phone. 'Well, I better get changed. Luckily we had a shower last night.'

We both manage to change before they arrive.

AFTER JESSICA AND TRUDY ARRIVE, we head to the police station for nine o'clock. I feel anxious about Sheila finding us a missing puzzle. I am hoping the boy left us some kind of clue to finding out who grew and sold drugs.

THE FOUR OF us are standing around the black bag that holds the body parts. Sheila is already in her scrubs preparing to carry out a forensic examination.

I have not seen her perform her job before. She is in her own little world as she leans on the desk and stares at the unopen bag.

Eventually, Sheila unzips the bag slowly as if the package is fragile as she shows respect for the dead. She asks us to leave her by herself as she begins her work.

SHEILA GENTLY TAKES out the pieces of his body and lays them out on the desk. She lays out Daniel Harris's remains in order from feet to head. This does not make her squirm or make her feel ill. However, she can imagine that if this happened to one of their kids, she would want her husband to find the person and kill them.

When she has finished laying out his parts, everything is there. Nothing appears to be missing.

The body is well preserved from the airtight freezer container it stayed in for almost forty years. The skin is leathery and discoloured from age.

Sheila is methodical and always begins from the feet and slowly examines her way up.

The feet can tell her a lot about a person, like the way he walked or if he took care of himself by how well his nails are groomed. There is nothing obvious. She can see that the feet and the rest of the body were cut with a serrated edge like a wood saw.

The shins and calves are examined next with nothing obvious to report.

She checks for bruises or broken skin caused by a tight grip with nails digging in or hit by a hard object. There is no sign of injury.

Sheila now checks the thighs for similar marks. She notices nothing.

It takes Sheila two hours to do a normal autopsy but then she spends an extra hour going into further detailed examination to allow for any missed signs or evidence to be collected.

It is not until she reaches the chest, which has been dissected in four pieces, that she can see the rib cage is slightly pressed in. She imagines that a knee would have caused the fractures, with the boy being held down. She has seen a few similar cases of damage in the past. Her mind conjures up a vision of how the person would have been on top of him trying to silence his scream. The killer would have been worried that nearby walkers or hikers could hear the boy scream. She cannot find any other marks on the boy's torso, such as a puncture wound from a knife or other sharp object.

She now checks what she can of the neck. It is hard to determine how much of the neck is easy to examine. There is dried aged blood faintly coating the skin. She can manage to determine that Daniel had been strangled. The skin is broken, and she can just make out that the throat had been crushed. She checks for any foreign skin cells left behind by the killer. It is very tricky to find as the cell will be very small and hard to see amongst the blood. Skin can rub off as friction is created. She only spends a few minutes before checking his head.

She is confident of finding specks in his hair and maybe marks on his skull. She can see that his killer tried to make his facial features unrecognisable. But she can guess that he could not go through with it, losing the courage to saw through. As per usual, specks of grass and dirt are found, which is to be expected. No fracture or broken bones are found around the crown, side or back.

The mouth and teeth are examined for any skin tissue caused by Daniel biting the attacker, a natural reaction to get the person off them. She is in luck as she finds a piece of skin in-between his lower molars. She is quick to use a pair of surgical tweezers to put it inside a specimen bottle.

Almost an hour and a half in, she checks his fingernails for skin as well, knowing that he would have scratched the person. Not only does she find flakes of skin, but blood is also found under his nails. This would suggest that he broke the person's skin while scratching them.

When she is finished with the first phase, she begins from the feet again and makes a more thorough search for anything she may have missed the first time.

JESSICA, Trudy and I have been waiting upstairs having a menial conversation. I finally told them about what happened last night. They found it hilarious and wished they could have been there. I thought they would sympathise, but they just kept asking me to tell the story again in case I missed something.

I notice Jessica staring at me differently like she is trying to read me. I wonder if I were younger and single, if I would make a pass at her like she did earlier in the week. I do find her pretty and innocent. At the same time, I would not feel comfortable dating a white girl in a town like this, being stared at as the only mixed couple in the town.

Trudy interrupts our eye contact when she suggests heading back downstairs for the results. I check the time to see that my wife has taken close to two hours.

SHEILA SEES us walk in and says, 'Ah, good timing. I have finished processing the body.'

I notice the remains are fully exposed and check with Jessica, 'Jessica, are you okay with this?'

Jessica gasps briefly and says, 'I'm fine. Was not expecting to see his body. Please, carry on. I'll focus on writing.'

Trudy is keen on her findings; 'What did you conclude?'

Sheila gives her professional opinion with pause for thought. 'After making a detailed assessment, the cause of death was strangulation. But the boy did not give up without a fight. I found fragments of skin cells under his fingernails. He was a fighter as I also found skin in between his lower teeth. There were no other marks apart from when they tried to dispose of his body.'

I have a question which may sound silly; 'Did they try to do what they did while he was alive?'

Sheila does not see my question as stupid. 'No. The cuts were precise. Imagine if you were being attacked alive. You would be fighting with the person, so, the cuts would be jagged, and there would be blood everywhere. Here, the cuts are straight and not lacerated. If you come closer, you can see where his neck has marks which are consistent with strangulation.'

Trudy is keen to know where the samples are. 'Where have you put the skin cells? I want to test the DNA on them.'

Sheila points to the side where there are plastic pots. Trudy continues with her work leaving Jessica and me.

As I observe the body, something catches my eye. 'Sheila, what is that in his left hand? Is it a wound from the struggle?'

Sheila has a blank look on her face. 'Let me see. I missed this. I thought it was just discoloured. Jessica, can you pass me the magnifying glass near Trudy?'

Jessica eventually sees it and passes it over. 'Here. What is it?'

Sheila takes a long look, then says, 'It appears to be ink. A drawing.'

I quickly stand next to her and use the magnifying glass, 'I think this is a drawing. It looks like a tree by the shape of it.'

Sheila is puzzled, 'Why would someone sketch a picture on their palm? A phone number or name would normally be written on a hand.'

I have a light bulb moment; 'I think he was sending a clue for the police to pick up.'

Jessica has had a week to understand how I think, and she can see I have an idea. 'Come out and say it.'

I keep my thoughts to myself but say, 'I think I know a way to find who his killer or killers were and confirm what he witnessed. I think Daniel has helped us break the case single-handedly.'

Trudy stops what she is doing and turns round. 'What did you just say?'

Sheila can also see that I feel we have solved the case. 'This symbol on his hand has solved the crime.'

I smile almost gleefully but remain cautious. 'I don't want to jump the boat. But I think I can solve his murder tomorrow. Trudy, carry on with the DNA testing. Then feed all the results through the police mainframe. If this person has never been arrested, he will still come up. Just trust me.'

Trudy knows what I mean but is puzzled by my conclusion.

Jessica has a sudden thought; 'The man that Daniel was startled by in the video.'

I do not respond and go to see the sheriff.

24

FURTHER QUESTIONS

I open Sheriff Bob's office door without announcing myself. He is surprised and sarcastically welcomes me in.

I briefly apologise without meaning it. 'I have a quick question.'

Sheriff Bob is still sarcastic, 'Come in. Do you want a coffee? Take a seat.'

I ignore him and say, 'Great. Back in 1982, did you know the kids' favourite haunts?'

Sheriff Bob has a blank expression. 'Why are you asking me this?'

I grow impatient and insist, 'Just answer the question. Did you keep a track of all the kids' hangouts?'

Sheriff Bob is still confused but answers my question; 'Yes! There were only so many places where they could go.'

I heave a sigh of relief and tell him, 'There is one more thing I need you to do.'

Sheriff Bob sighs, 'What?'

I have an idea that sounds crazy but makes sense; 'I need to be somewhere today. But I need to make a phone call to you, here, in your office, and I will need you to be able to let everyone hear that conversation. You think you could somehow do that?'

Sheriff Bob is cautious; 'What are you up to?'

'Just ask the question. Are you able to do that?'

Sheriff Bob reluctantly agrees to do me the favour. 'You better keep me in the loop with your hair-brained scheme.'

I smile with a little bit of excitement and say, 'Will do. I have to get going. I need to be somewhere.'

As I leave his office and close the door behind me, I hear my cell phone ring. I can see it is Senator Charleston and think, 'good timing.'

. . .

I ANSWER the phone with enthusiasm. 'This is good timing. I think I have solved the case.'

Senator Charles stops me in my tracks. 'I have phoned on a different matter. It is not to put pressure on you. Something has come up.'

I do not like the tone of his distressed voice; 'Say it.'

Senator Charleston stutters, 'It's Alex Jefferson's execution. It is taking place tomorrow.'

I have that sinking feeling. 'When did this happen?'

Senator Charleston is frantic with worry. 'It was accelerated some time ago. Only been made aware of it now. I'm not expecting a miracle, but how close are you to solving this?'

I realise he did not hear me the first time, so I repeat, 'I think I can solve this by tomorrow morning. When is the execution?'

Senator Charleston rifles through the pile of papers on his desk. 'It will be at eleven o'clock in the morning.'

I work backwards in my mind. 'I need to tie up loose ends by ten-thirty. Give me enough time to tell you and then cancel the execution. It will also mean providing this to a judge to rubber-stamp my argument.'

Senator Charleston is still worried and pleads, 'Promise me you will call me as soon as you put this case to bed.'

I almost forget to tell him that we have found the body. 'One bit of good news. We found Daniel Harris. He has already been autopsied. We know how he died.'

The senator goes quiet on the phone, and I can just about hear him whimper, 'Thank God. Thank God. Now, I know you can save Alex's life. Please tell me that you can find a suspect.'

'That is what I am about to do. So, I have something concrete to put in front of the judge.'

Senator Charleston does not want to hold me up any longer and hangs up.

I forget my original plan to go for a drive to find my suspect. I rush downstairs to talk to Trudy and ask her for an estimated time for completing her results.

JESSICA IS STANDING over Trudy and Sheila as they tinker with the equipment to produce answers. I interrupt their flow to get an answer.

I stand next to Trudy and make her stop what she is doing. 'I need a miracle. How quick can your machines produce the DNA evidence?'

Trudy has to think on her feet. 'I have only just put it in the analysis machine. You are looking at two hours at least. What is it?'

I check my watch to see it is close to midday. 'That will be two o'clock. How long will it take to cross-match it against the database?'

Trudy has to make an educated guess; 'If the person is in the CODIS database like you say they are, about two hours.'

I think about the time then being four o'clock. 'Okay. That gives me four hours to make a trip. I need to call one of Daniel's three friends. I have twenty-six hours to have everything sown up. Give me a call when you have the results. Only the three of us will know. I don't want any of you to let the sheriff know. Got that?'

The three of them stare at me with intrigue. I ask Trudy if I can borrow her car for a couple of hours and she hands over the keys.

I run out of the police station to the SUV. As I hastily drive away, I get on the phone to the first person in my head.

I hear William on the phone. 'Hi. This is Stoane. I spoke to you four days ago about Daniel. I need your help and I'm coming over to see you now.'

I struggle to keep to the speed limit as I race to his office to pick him up.

When I arrive at William's office, he is already waiting outside for me. He gets in the car, and I screech the tyres and zoom out of the car park.

I can remember how to get to Cove Forest Road from my memory of when Jessica first drove us there. William is nervous about my driving, and I do not make conversation as my mind is swimming with the thought of a hunch.

When we reach the road, I almost forget and slam on the brakes before yanking the steering wheel to go left. The back end swings out as I drive into the road.

I eventually begin to slow down as we reach the end of the road to park up.

When we get out, I ask William to confirm the tree that they used to climb when they were kids. He is puzzled and curious as to why I want him to take me to the tree.

After a couple of minutes, we arrive. I search the base of the trunk trying to find a covered hole or gap between the roots. There is nothing.

William asks what I am trying to find, but I do not acknowledge his question. My next instinct is to look up at the branches. I judge how high up the branches begin. The thought of climbing the tree in my forties does not thrill me. For a brief second, I consider asking William to go up.

I think about where else Daniel could have meant before I consider clambering up the tree. Nothing comes to mind and so I make my attempt to go up the tree. There are no stumps to use as footholds. I have to rely on my shoes giving me grip and my arms taking my weight. I slip a couple of times as I hoist myself up. It takes me about five minutes to finally reach the branches. I take a moment to get my breath back. I glance down and cannot believe how high up I am. I must be about fifteen feet up.

I feel with my hands for any holes or objects, thinking that it has been thirty-eight years and the weather and elements could have destroyed the evidence. I am about to give up hope thinking that my theory is just that, hopeless, when I finally grab something.

I quickly pull it away from the base of the cluster of branches.

I CLIMB BACK DOWN before I examine what I have found. It is covered in what I assume is a white handkerchief.

A couple of feet from the ground, I jump away from the tree trunk. I almost twist my foot but manage to safely get down.

William sees there is something in my hand. 'What is that? How did you know that something was up there?'

I carefully unravel the handkerchief to see what it is. 'Daniel left a clue.'

William is perplexed. 'How do you know that when you have not met him or found his body?'

I forget that we have kept that quiet, so just say, 'I'll explain later. For now, I will take you back to work.'

William notices the black book straight away. 'That is Daniel's little black book that he carried with him all the time. How did you know he kept it there?'

I eventually tell him, swearing him to secrecy; 'We found him. We are not making it public as I do not want to spook the killer. If you tell anyone, I'll have you arrested and press charges for interfering with a police investigation.'

William is spooked by my threat. 'Of course. I didn't really think you find him. Will you eventually tell me where you found him?'

I give my word; 'Everyone will know. But his parents first. Everyone will know come Wednesday. For now, keep it to yourself.'

William gestures in agreement and then I drive him back to the office.

I AM keen to drop William at his office so I can go be alone to open the little black book. I do not make conversation for fear of accidentally discussing the case.

William notices me being fidgety with my free hand clutching the book strongly. He does not say anything, but I can see that he is curious to find out what could be in the book that is making me anxious.

The five-minute drive seems like ten minutes.

When I reach his office, I kindly hurry him out of the car. As soon as he closes the door, I zoom off and drive somewhere where I can be alone.

I decide to drive back to my trailer where I know I will not be disturbed.

WHEN I DRIVE inside the trailer park, I almost drive into the side of my trailer as I slam on the brakes and the tyres screech to a halt.

25

FINALLY DISCOVERING THE KILLER

After I get inside, I find myself sat at the kitchen table studying the front cover of the book. I am scared that the book will not identify his killer; that this journey to find it is a waste of effort. At the same time, Alex Jefferson is relying on this to free him.

I decide to pour a glass of rum first before I open the pages to see his last entry towards the back of the book.

It is surprising how the black book has survived all these years, despite rain, frost and nature. I imagine Daniel never expected the police to take this long to find his body.

I gulp the entire contents and then pour out another glass.

Before I flick through the first few pages, I read his notes and thoughts from the beginning. I can see straight away that he would have wanted to be a cop. The details he has written is an interpretation of how he thought cops would write a report. His notes include day, date, time and incident. It makes me emotional getting an immediate understanding of how Daniel methodically thought; his approach to investigating trivial incidents, such as the paperboy not dropping off the paper properly and the neighbour poorly placing his garbage out the front. These minute things had been written to a professional police standard. I can imagine he had a children's book on how to be a detective.

I skim through a couple more pages and notice he began writing his thoughts down on what he had witnessed. It reads like a black and white detective film. His description is very articulate when describing his mood and opinion.

. . .

AFTER I FINISH GETTING an understanding of Daniel's character, I feel that I know him. I now prepare myself to find out what he saw that made him lose his life so young.

I feel knots in my stomach as I find out if he has written a name. I do not know on what page the last notes are written, so I go from the back and flick the pages until I see writing.

There is an entry for 27th October 1982 which makes the hairs on the back of my neck raise. He also wrote the day as being Wednesday. He has written that he saw a truck for the seventh time driving past Cove Forest Road. He wrote that the truck had a distinct image on the number plate. I can see a sketch of what he saw.

The drawing is of a typical six-year-old. I find it hard to know what the image is meant to be. I study it while trying to match my own ideas to the picture. I have a light bulb moment when I realise that it is of two wings, like a bird or an angel. At first, I assumed it to be the inside of an apple or a poorly drawn butterfly. Either type of drawing would not be used on a number plate.

I read on to find out that Daniel had figured out where the truck had been driving to. I can see that being so young, he had no idea that he had seen a cannabis crop. In his book, he describes odd plants that appear like over-grown weeds. Daniel found it strange why someone would help spread weeds on a crop. He thought people were trying to sabotage a farmer's field.

I finally see names written down based on previous conversations he had overheard. There are three names that I have not heard of before. However, it confirms that they must be the people who played a part in killing the boy.

EVEN THOUGH IT is in the middle of the day, I pour myself a glass of rum and down it in one. My mind is conjuring up an image from the pages of what he saw and the repercussions.

The case is beginning to affect me, and I imagine if one of my boys had been harmed like him. Daniel only wanted to do what he knew to be right; Informing on the three men at the police station.

As I go to down another drink, the thought of the truck and the three men stops me. I put the over-filled glass down and rush over to my crazy wall. I cannot get the truck out of my head. I realise that one of the three incidents that happened on the night included a burnt-out truck. It is too much of a coincidence; the truck described in the book must be the same one reported in the newspaper.

Everything begins to fit into place about that night. The three men stole a car to kidnap the boy and then abandoned the car where the cabin is, deep in the woods. Something happened for the car not to be destroyed, but that is not important. The cabin had been wiped clean and the truck must have been set on fire to hide the evidence of it ever being used for the drug operation.

Also, I bet the DNA found on the baseball cap and on his body will match up with the three names in the book. I have the evidence now that Alex Jefferson is innocent. It is as clear as day. I need to get to the police station to cross-reference against Trudy's results and the database.

When I arrive back at the police station basement, Sheila, Trudy and Jessica are wondering where I have been.

I realise it is close to four o'clock already and Trudy has reached her findings. The database has brought up the persons who share the DNA samples.

Now I know who they are, I ask if one of them happens to be a police officer and mention the three names from the book. All three women are shocked that I already know the answer.

I take Daniel's book out of my coat pocket and ask, 'You know when we were asking about the drawing on his palm?'

All three acknowledge my question.

I continue, 'Well, I figured it was the tree that he and his three friends hung around at the time. It took a while to find what I assumed was his little black book. It bothered me that it was not found in his possession, even though his body was naked. Also, I felt that he had placed it in a safe place in case anything happened to him. He must have known that something bad was going to happen. I'm guessing he hid it before he came to the police station that night.'

Trudy motions me to give her the black book. 'So, these three men are the real suspects?'

I gently nod my head. 'Now we have the evidence that puts them at the cabin, the stolen car and the murder; I want to surprise them. Also, I need to get a confession out of them. I want all three to get life. All three will blame the other.'

Sheila can see what I have in mind and wants to speak to me in private.

We leave the basement and go outside at the back of the police station. Sheila wants to know what I am going to do.

I cannot make eye contact as it will mean breaking the law. 'I'm not a cop anymore. The people here and the sheriff will turn a blind eye. Bob already asked me to make sure I get justice for the boy.'

Sheila is worried that I may go too far and says, 'I don't want you going to jail for them. You have solved the case now. It is time to go home.'

I cannot do that, so I tell her, 'I want closure. Then, I need to see his parents and tell them that we got his killers before the media catch wind. You do know this will be a nationwide story.'

Sheila sighs, 'I want you safe. You don't know what these men are capable of. They were drug dealers.'

I give her reassurance; 'I will make sure the sheriff is there before any crazy stuff happens. I'm the only one who can do this. I do not have a uniform or a boss to report to. I am going to do this my way.'

Sheila has no choice but to accept my decision. 'Okay. Just don't do anything stupid like kill them. They need to stand trial.'

I promise her, 'I will just probably maim them. Cut off a finger or an ear.'

Sheila gives me a mean stare. I assure her that I am joking.

We walk back inside and let Trudy and Jessica know that I will be going alone from here on. I ask to borrow Trudy's car again to head to the cabin. I want the three men to be held accountable for the heinous crime.

Jessica feels compelled to hug me and orders me to be safe and call for backup if it gets hairy. Trudy suggests that I carry a radio and ask for one from the sheriff. I think that is a good idea and I tell her that I will.

I go to see Bob to let him know that we solved the case.

Bob is pouring himself a coffee by the coffee station in the open office. I guess his own is empty.

Bob sees me and has a different curious stare. 'Is this a private conversation?'

I check to see that no one is prying on our conversation before saying, 'I need a radio, some kind of recording device and you on standby.'

Bob is intrigued; 'You've solved the crime. Are you going to tell me what you're going to do?'

'I think it is better that you don't know. I also need a car battery and spark leads. Just don't ask.'

Bob is happy to supply all the equipment, 'Give me ten minutes. Sure, you don't want me to come with you?'

I think he will scare the suspects off, so I decline his offer; 'If they catch wind that you are out there with me, they won't turn up. I'm going to call you when I'm ready. I want you to talk out loud for everyone to hear in the police station. You'll know what to say. Then I want you to listen in on the confession. As soon as I get it, you come and arrest them. Make it official.'

Bob is more than happy to go along with my plan, 'Sure you don't want me to come? I can park out of sight and be ready to assist.'

I briefly think about his offer then say, 'Thanks, but I do not want them to have any inkling that they are going to be set up.'

With that, I head out to the cabin alone.

26

THE TRUTH FINALLY COMES OUT

It is past five o'clock and I have already set up the living room of the log cabin. I managed to find a car battery from one of the cars impounded at the police station.

I have no weapon on me, but I do not feel that I need one. They will likely come armed, but I am prepared for that.

There is no light on the outside veranda, so I have the element of surprise when they come in. There is only one way in so I cannot be ambushed. I have used the freezer, which Daniel's remains were in, to block the back door. I also found a doorstop and wedged that under the unit so it cannot be pushed back.

There are no electric lights, so it is nice and dark which gives me the upper hand.

I am almost ready to make the call and get the man in the station to overhear the conversation and come up. I know he will bring his two other associates as backup.

I GO OUTSIDE to find better reception to call Sheriff Bob on the phone. Before I do, I test out the radio to make sure he can receive my call. Bob answers straight away and wonders why I did not use the landline as agreed. I quickly explain that I wanted to make sure the receivers worked okay before I called him.

My cell phone rings, and I see it is Sheila, 'Why are you calling?'

Sheila is apprehensive about the plan. 'Wanted to make sure you are okay up there. Have you made the call?'

I am growing impatient and say, 'I was about to before you interrupted. Now, get off the phone.'

Sheila wants to say one more thing; 'Trudy and Jessica are with me. They are waiting anxiously.'

I roll my eyes as I sigh, 'No kidding. Now get off the phone. I am about to call the sheriff.'

My hands begin to shake with adrenaline as I dial Bob's number. This is it.

I hear the dial tone for a few seconds before he picks up. 'Hi, is that the sheriff?'

Sheriff Bob elevates his voice, 'This is Bob speaking. Who is this?'

I pretend to be an anomalous caller. 'I went hiking and came across a cabin in the woods. I think someone has broken into it.'

Sheriff Bob plays along with my call, 'Right. What seems to be the problem?'

I struggle to come up with a lame reason, 'I think there is something suspicious. I want to have a police officer come down and check things are alright.'

Sheriff Bob knows his cue as he continues to speak loudly, 'So, you're telling me that you think something sinister is taking place in the cabin?'

I reiterate my concern, 'I think there is something inside that could be suspicious.'

Sheriff Bob glances at his staff to figure out who could be reacting, 'So, you think there is something suspicious inside. At the back of the cabin. Well, we are a little stretched. No one can come out for at least a couple of hours.'

I finish the conversation, 'Well, I can't wait for that long. I will be heading home.'

Sheriff Bob understands and goes on, 'So, you are going home now. Then I will have a police officer come out that way in the next two hours.'

We both hang up.

A MAN in the office has heard the whole conversation and has kept himself discrete by pretending to be finding something in the filing cabinet.

He has panic all over his face at the thought of Daniel's body still being in the freezer after all those years. He never thought he would have to move the body after almost forty years.

When he finishes browsing through the files, he closes the drawer and sneaks out of the office. He walks out into the lobby and takes out his mobile. He calls one of his two old business partners. While waiting for him to pick up, he checks that no one is around.

He is getting nervous and agitated as he waits for an answer. 'What took you long to pick up?'

The person on the other end of the phone is blasé; 'What is the panic? Slow down.'

'I think the boy's body will be discovered. I told you we should have gone back and finished the job.'

The person orders him to calm down. 'The plan worked. That black guy took the fall. They will assume that he put it there. It will never come back to us.'

He thinks differently and says, 'It just so happens that some n—-r ex-cop was sent here to solve the case. Isn't it a bit of a coincidence that the body may be found now?'

The person exerts his voice, 'Woah. What investigation? They re-opened the case. On what grounds?'

He has no idea and only heard snippets of conversation. 'All I know is that he came here a week ago. Said something about a congressman trying to raise his profile by showing an interest in finding the missing boy.'

'So what? Why are you calling? I haven't heard from you in years. Now, you are calling, panicking about some dumb retired cop. What can he do that was already sorted out forty years ago?'

He tries to assure him that they have a problem on their hands. 'I have a bad feeling about this. New DNA technology. They could find something on the body and realise it wasn't that n—-r. I'm scared. The sheriff is sending some cops to the cabin tonight.'

The person soon realises why he is stressing. 'S--t. You're kidding. The body is too old. If there was any DNA off us, it will be long gone.'

He knows how good new equipment can pick up samples that are decades old and insists, 'I'm telling you. If there is fly s—t on that body, they will find it. I cleaned everywhere in that cabin except for the boy. He bit you and clawed at us. S—t, they could perform DNA on his cap. That has been in storage here all that time. I should have destroyed it.'

The person reminds him of their plan; 'If you did that, they wouldn't suspect the lonely visitor coming into town. It would have led to us.'

He remembers another thing; 'S—t. They found the car we used to kidnap him. They must have searched for evidence.'

The person has no idea why he is not on top of it. 'And? Why aren't you following them and asking questions about where they are? You're a cop. They wouldn't have questioned you.'

He bites his tongue. 'Look! I didn't expect someone to go hitch-hiking finding the cabin. It is in the middle of nowhere. No one knows that place exists. Hence why we grew drugs there and made a fortune. Until that kid poked his nose into our business. Like I said, something hinkey is going on. The case is open and now the cabin is found. I don't like this. I think we should go up there and finish the job.'

The person thinks for a second then says, 'Okay, who is going to let Jim know?'

I TEST that the battery with the 'jump start' leads works by tapping the metal draining tray in the kitchen. I wait for a spark as an indication. A few orange flares appear so I am happy.

I grab three chairs that are in the room and place them next to each other. I have rope to tie them up and all I need is a trap. I want to disarm them, and I have a great idea I picked up from being in the army. It will disable them instantly.

IT IS COMING CLOSE to six o'clock and I assume they will be here anytime soon to carry out their task. From years of being in the police, I know they will be allowing for half an hour to theoretically dispose of his remains in the acid. One thing I do not know is what they will do with the drum. Either way, their plan will not be carried out as they will not find his remains.

I can hear a very faint noise of a vehicle and twigs cracking from underneath the wheels. It is showtime.

I HEAR the car stop and see the headlights shining into the cabin. I crouch by the right side of the door under the window ledge. I made a hole in the wall earlier, under the window. I wait, poised, as I hear their footsteps coming closer.

Their heavy steps thud on the wooden floor of the veranda. I can hear them talking amongst themselves. One of them has noticed liquid underneath their feet and curse what it could be. With that, I shove a naked wire into the water puddle and all three get an instant electric shock. I wait until they collapse from the excruciating pain. One by one, they crash to the floor.

ALL THREE MEN are tied up in the chairs and I have attached the jump leads to the first person. I have clipped them to his ears. I want to give him a massive headache. The other two will feel the pain when my first subject can no longer cope. I have used wet cloths to avoid their ear lobes hurting as much and waking him up.

Their rifles and a handgun are emptied of bullets, and I've also dismantled them and chucked them in the steel drum out the back. They are being eroded by the bottles of acid.

In turn, I splash water at them from an old paint pot to wake them up. They all wake up in surprise that they are tied up and with mouths gagged.

I turn to my first test subject. 'I am going to tell you a little about my background. I was a bit of a rogue officer learning original techniques to torture an enemy. Surprisingly, none of them were commissioned by my superior. It even got to a point that I was asked to leave. So, I joined the police force and kept my nose clean until one day I had a dilemma. There was a suspect who killed my brother in-law's wife. It was proven that he was the only person who could have done it. But there was a catch twenty-two. My brother-in-law wasn't innocent himself. If he acted as the witness, he would bring shame to his family. So, I had to get it out of the suspect who would not talk. That meant I had to improvise. It got me fired but the confession got him imprisoned.'

Marty panics, 'You can't do this. You're a cop.'

27

I'M GOING TO ASK A BUNCH OF QUESTIONS

I can see Marty trembling as he stares into my eyes. It feels weird to find out that he, James and the assistant cop, Timothy, are the killers.

I wonder why Nancy is not involved and if he has knowledge of what they did. I also wonder why they gave the false witness statements so close to the truth. At the same time, Timothy would know that if you keep the story simple, you will never deviate from it. By telling the truth but conjuring up a made-up description of the kidnapping, it pointed to Alex Jefferson.

I shrug off his comment. 'I'm not a cop. I am just looking into the case when requested by your ex-resident, Senator Charleston. Now, I am going to ask a bunch of questions. If I feel you are not cooperating or are lying to me, I will give your head a slight buzz. Nod if you understand.'

Marty slowly and nervously gestures. 'What do you want to know?'

The other two try to hush Marty and shake with anger.

I crouch down to the battery and hold one of the leads in preparation to attaching it to the pin, 'How did you know to say that you saw a dark figure drive the black car with the boy in it?'

The other two get louder trying to get Marty to stop.

Marty begins to talk, 'There are no black folks in this town. He stood out like a sore thumb. He was a wanderer. It was nothing personal...'

I attach the cable to the pin and watch Marty convulse as the electric charge shoots through his ear lobes and rattles his brain. I leave it on for a few seconds and then release it.

Marty shouts out while spitting, 'What was that for?!'

I give him an explanation; 'I didn't like your tone. He was heading to university to study medicine. He could have saved countless lives with his skills. But you took that away. It could just have been a cold case with a mystery in the air. Now, tell me if Nancy knew any of this?'

Marty pauses for a second then says, 'No...'

I sense hesitation and connect the cable again but leave it for a bit longer. Marty's body spasms as he screams at the top of his lungs. His pain does not faze me.

I wait for him to recover before I continue; 'Does Nancy know about your fun night out?'

Marty, subdued from the torture, finally admits, 'Yes. Yes.'

I have finished with Marty and now go to question Timothy. As I go to clip the same cables I used on Marty, he wriggles and shouts out curse words at me beginning with 'F' and 'C'. It does not rile me but gives me plenty of ammunition to make him feel.

I punch him in the face to shut him up and then attach leads without the damp cloths. I hate a bad cop.

I watch him try to pretend that his ear lobes are not stinging, 'You are a tough cookie. I think you were the one who graffitied my hire car. I like the way you mis-spelled N—-r to throw me off the scent. Think that it was some uneducated redneck. Well, that is the least of your problems. I want to know how you knew where Alex was living and how you broke in without a trace.'

Timothy tries to spit in my face, but I move out of the way in time. 'F—K you!'

I connect the lead again and leave it on for a good thirty seconds. 'That gotta hurt. Give me a number between one and ten. Ten being the worst.'

Timothy only curses, 'F—k you, N—-r. C--t.'

I am impressed with his vocabulary, 'Wow. I wish I had gone to your school. I need you to tell me so I can record it on this device and incriminate you. So, speak clearly into the mic.'

Timothy continues with his foul language, 'You are a F—king c--t.'

I jam on the cable and turn away to walk towards the window. Then, I rest my back against the pane. I see Marty and James in shock as Timothy reels in pain and spasms viciously. I think I can smell wee and maybe excrement.

I take my time walking over to the battery and unplugging the cable. 'I will get your friend James to speak on your behalf and besides, we have DNA from all three of you all over the boy. If it was not for your genius idea to dissolve Daniel's body in acid, you would have tried to clean him up. Also, DNA analysis was not around then for you to think that far ahead.'

James is now petrified, and he blabbers like a five-year-old kid owning up to eating out of the cookie jar. He tells the whole story about how they made thousands of dollars growing cannabis and being the number one supplier in the town. Also, how they supplied in neighbouring towns.

Daniel had spotted their truck and began to show an interest in where they were driving to. He confirms that on the night they murdered him, they stole a saw and the car from a garage. It made sense why James, Marty and Nancy lied about parking opposite the police station, with Timothy backing up their claim. Between the four of them, they provided their own alibi without anyone noticing.

I knew the burglary of the house had something to do with the murder but did know how or why. It makes sense now, as they had to find a saw. If they bought it in a shop, it could have implicated them.

IT IS a good hour or so before I feel I have enough evidence on the recording device. I made a point of not recording the noise of grown men screaming, to make the confession admissible in court.

Soon after seven o'clock, I can hear the wailing noise of several police cars screaming through the woods.

I leave them tied up and casually walk out of the cabin to greet them. Sheriff Bob gives me a huge grin as he heard the whole thing via the radio. He holds his hand out to me and I eventually shake his hand.

I tell him that Trudy, Sheila and I have gathered the evidence that ties the three men to the murder and the growing of weed. I ask about Nancy and before I finish my sentence, he tells me that a cop car is already on the way to arrest him.

I ask him what time the courthouse opens tomorrow so I can present the confession and forensic evidence to exonerate Alex Jefferson.

Sheriff Bob shakes his head and says, 'No. I'm going with you. I will do all the talking and get your man freed. Thanks for everything, Stoane. I guess I now know why your parents named you Stoane Cold. You really are cold.'

I chortle at his comment. 'I was never a boy scout. I needed a confession fast. Alex is going to get the electric chair tomorrow. I need to be there before eleven o'clock.'

Sheriff Bob comes across as scared when he says, 'The court opens at ten o'clock. It will take at least thirty minutes to show our findings and then sign a form to pass over to the prison.'

I think outside the box, 'How about emailing or faxing?'

Sheriff Bob gestures a negative response. 'This is backwards. It has to be an original.'

I do not bother trying to argue for a change. I leave him and his colleagues to clean up the mess I have left and head back to my wife, Trudy and Jessica. I am keen to have an early night in bed.

IT IS nine o'clock in the morning. Both my wife and I are already dressed and waiting impatiently for the sheriff to pick me up and head to the court.

I could not sleep a wink. I tossed and turned, worried that I would oversleep and allow an innocent man to die. Sheila had trouble sleeping as she could feel me turning under the blanket.

My stomach has knots and so only Sheila had some toast and coffee. She can see how important this is to me and all she can do is hold my hand and reassure me.

I appreciate her being here; she is proud to have helped me and the police to find concrete evidence of the boy's murderer.

A LITTLE AFTER quarter past nine, the sheriff finally arrives and does not bother coming in. He waits by the front door for me to come to him. I kiss my wife on her forehead as I leave to go with him to get a pardon.

The five-minute drive feels like half an hour as I keep checking the time on my watch. We do not make conversation as I have too much worry on my mind. It is down to me to make sure Alex does not die in the next two hours. My palms are beginning to get sweaty from the nerves.

As WE ARRIVE outside the courthouse, I see Trudy is here already with Jessica. I guess she is going to provide the new evidence to reinforce Alex's release.

The four of us go inside and head to the judge's chamber.

I CONSCIOUSLY CHECK the time every couple of minutes, knowing that we have a half an hour's drive to get to the prison.

It is a long walk as it is along a hallway to reach the judge's office.

SHERIFF BOB DOES NOT BOTHER KNOCKING on the door as he barges in apologising to the judge for our abruptness.

The man is in his late sixties with white hair and a bald crown. He is still wearing his black robe.

Sheriff Bob explains our presence. 'Judge Palmer, we need you to sign a pardon to release a prisoner.'

Judge Palmer is startled by our entrance and demands, 'What is this about?'

Sheriff Bob turns to Trudy. 'We have new evidence that proves that an inmate is innocent. Trudy here has the proof of who did. There were three men involved. I need you to make a pardon before he is killed.'

Judge Palmer is slowly taking this in, 'What case is this?'

I interrupt. 'I have been investigating the disappearance of Daniel Harris. We found his body and that led us to the real killers. There is an innocent

man who is going to be executed at eleven o'clock this morning. Sign the
pardon so we can get there in time.'

Judge Palmer glances at Bob and accepts my word. 'Okay. But I want a full
explanation of what is happening.'

It takes Judge Palmer a while to complete an official letter. His eyes are
failing, and he takes his time with typing. I keep checking my watch thinking
that we are not going to make it.

When he finally completes the letter and prints it off, my watch says
twenty to eleven.

28

IN THE NICK OF TIME

It is Alex Jefferson's last day on earth. As you can imagine, he did not sleep at all last night. He kept stirring awake, imagining being in the chair already. Sometimes, he felt as if he had already died and wondered where he is now.

You prefer to be awake to make the most of what life you have left. You have all the time to sleep when you are no longer alive.

ALEX HAS BEEN UP for a while but has no idea how long. He has been too nervous and scared to eat breakfast. All he has had is water to keep hydrated.

He is keen to know what time it is as there is no clock. He guesses from the light strobing in from a window bar high up, and the time he has been awake, that it must be after ten o'clock.

There have been no prison guards around since being offered anything he wants as a last meal. The place feels abandoned like he is the only person in prison. There is not even a sound of clanging prison doors or a jingle of key chains. He feels like he could somehow break out of his cell and escape.

It is not long before one of the guards comes to see him. The guard asks him if there is going to be anyone who wants to see him, but deep down, he knows that no one is going to see him and give him comfort. Alex has chosen not to see a priest to help save his soul from hell.

He begins to wonder what it will feel like to be injected and if there will be pain as he slowly dies. He wonders if he will fall asleep first or if it is instant. Whether it will feel like he is offered local anaesthetic or feel like poison is coursing through his veins.

Eventually, he stops himself from pondering on the thought and asks the guard for the time. He does not respond to his question at first, as he is here to take him for his last walk.

Aʟᴇx ᴀsᴋs him for the time again and the guard reluctantly tells him that it is close to ten forty-five. He explains that he is here to walk him to the room. He does not use the term 'execution'.

The guard can see in Alex's eyes that he already has regret for harming the boy. He wonders why the black man came to see him a week ago. He did not think to ask Alex at the time.

The guard has found him to be a quiet gentle person despite his height and size. He never caused problems for the guards or made trouble with other inmates. He finds it hard to believe that he would harm a child.

Alex's wrists are handcuffed, and his ankles are chained as well. He follows the guard out of the cell and walks along a long shiny corridor.

He knows this is it and that with each step he takes, the further he is from his old life living in prison. It feels surreal for him as if he is having an out-of-body experience.

He wished that he could see his lover one more time, but he knows that the person would never come to see him. He wishes he had a photo of them, so he could see them as he slowly dies. Some kind of comfort that they are thinking of him.

Alex reflects on his life and wonders what it may have been like if he had not been framed for the disappearance of a local boy. He imagines himself being a doctor and working in Los Angeles where he dreamed of living. He thinks about whether he would have been married by now and potentially have children. Even though he has not seen the world in the past forty years, he has learned a lot from the guards who moan and form opinions on life outside the prison.

He has some regrets about not speaking out at the time by saying who he spent the night with. But a few seconds later, he quickly reminds himself why he never said anything.

Alex has his own demons from his past before he walked into Marion, but never told anyone about it except for his lover. A part of him feels that spending time in jail did not make up for what he did before Marion. He wonders if being executed will be the thing that makes him feel that he has received enough punishment to make up for the loss.

He feels that he has made peace with God for allowing one of his children to die. As he thinks about it, he sheds a tear feeling that he will soon be free.

.   .   .

TRUDY AND JESSICA trail behind Sheriff Bob and me as we rush to his police car. I check my watch and see that it is now ten to eleven. We are not going to make it.

I stand by the passenger door and lose hope of making it to the prison in time. It is an eight-minute drive, time to sign in and then rush to stop the execution.

Sheriff Bob is still hopeful. 'You are giving up already. You got this far. I can do it in five. And you're forgetting that I have a siren.'

Once again, I feel that we have a chance. 'Yes. You're right. What are we waiting for?'

Once we are in the car, Sheriff Bob screeches the tyres, leaving a trail of smoke behind us.

TRUDY AND JESSICA are stunned by the way Sheriff Bob is driving his car. The smoke from the tyres almost engulfs them and Trudy's car.

SHERIFF BOB IS BEGINNING to give him hope that we will make it. I notice that we are going at over a hundred miles an hour through the quiet roads of Marion town.

It is not long before we reach the gas station that I went to when arriving here. Sheriff Bob is driving so fast that we leave the tarmac as we reach the brow of a slight incline.

There are a few cars in front of us sticking to the speed limit of fifty miles an hour. Sheriff Bob overtakes three cars and manages to sneak back onto our side as a ten-tonne truck faces us. I hear the horn blow and the tyres screech with plumes of smoke funnelling from under the truck and trailer. I almost have a heart attack and turn round to see if there has been an accident.

I grip the dashboard like that will save my life, feeling my nails dig into the hard plastic.

WITH THE SPEED we are doing and from my memories of the journey to Marion, I figure we are two minutes away. I check my watch to see that it is close to eleven o'clock. I imagine Alex already being placed in the chair or upright against a medical bed.

It is not long before we reach the entrance to the prison. I imagine being held up at the gate preventing us from saving Alex. As I have thoughts of being asked a load of questions by the guard, Sheriff Bob does not take his foot off the gas. If anything, he slams the pedal to the metal, and I feel the car going faster. I soon realise he is not going to stop.

I close my eyes thinking that the barrier will win this fight. The next thing

I hear is a huge bang and feel that the engine has fallen out. The impact forces me to open my eyes and I see that we have already driven through the entrance. I hear the guard yelling at the top of his voice.

SHERIFF BOB HEADS towards reception and but veers off course and leaves me questioning his driving.

He shouts above the engine and road noise that he knows where the execution is going to take place. I agree that it is a good idea to go straight there.

Within seconds, we have almost reached the building. I prepare to get out as soon as we stop.

But just as I think Sheriff Bob is driving to the entrance of the building, I see us heading towards the wall. I stutter, asking him what he is doing. He asks if I have my seat belt on and I quickly check, knowing that I put it on before we left the courthouse. I yank the belt to see that it locks.

Sheriff Bob yells at me to brace myself and before I realise what he is about to do, we impact the wall.

I DO NOT KNOW if I passed out or everything happened so fast, but I suddenly find us inside the building with rubble coating the hood of the car. The windscreen has cracked but it did not shatter. The airbag deployed and I feel like my nose is broken. I quickly turn to Sheriff Bob to see that he is okay, and he gives me the thumbs up.

Once I know he is fine, I yell at him, 'What the f—k did you do that for? You could have killed us.'

Sheriff Bob begins coughing from the dust in the air. 'I had to do something to stop the execution. A knock on the door wouldn't have done anything. Besides, I thought you wanted to save this guy from execution.'

ONCE THE DUST LITERALLY SETTLES, it is soon apparent that we almost hit the spectators attending the event. We wiped out three rows of empty chairs in front of the visitors.

A couple of hours after crashing the party, we found out that they were about to put the needle in Alex's arm. If Sheriff Bob had not acted so quickly, he would have been dead for sure.

It is two o'clock now and Sheriff Bob did all the talking, explaining our action and showing the letter to pardon Alex Jefferson.

We are told that his execution will be cancelled, and he will be released in a few days' time. Alex is taken back to his original cell in the main prison. I wait for one of the guards to say it is okay to see him.

. . .

At about four o'clock, I ask Sheriff Bob if I can see him alone as I have some questions to ask. He says that he has to get us another car anyhow and so goes to make a phone call.

When I see Alex in his cell, I take a seat on the bottom bunk next to him. I can see in his eyes that he wanted to die. I leave it a few minutes before I ask him a personal question.

I make light of this morning's event; 'Wow, I have never seen such a bunch of scared spectators. You must have thought it was God who intervened.'

Alex nervously laughs but tries not to. 'I thought this was what hell was like. Did you find the person who killed that boy?'

I slowly nod, 'Yeah. I know why you did it. I can see it in your eyes. I saw it when I came to see you last week. I know you don't want to tell me, but eventually, I will find out.'

Alex pretends that I am reading into something that isn't there. 'You are looking too much into it.'

I tell him my thoughts, 'Something happened before you reached Marion. Something so bad, that you felt you should be punished for it. But, whatever you did, it did not carry a sentence. You thought being accused of another crime would compensate. You thought God had given you a second chance to suffer for whatever happened. And now, you're confused. Did God send us to save you, or did you spend forty years in jail for nothing?'

Alex shouts back, 'No! I deserved everything I got. It was God's punishment and he sent me here.'

I refuse to agree and say, 'The person that did not come out of the darkness to save your ass deserves to be here. You didn't do anything so bad that it warranted God punishing you for it. Whatever you did, that is on your conscience. If you deserved to be punished, you would have been for that. Not this.'

After I finish letting him know that I have an inkling of who he is protecting, I leave him.

As I walk out, I turn round to face him. 'One other thing. Hire the most expensive lawyer you can find.'

Alex is puzzled and asks, 'Why?'

I give a slight smile. 'Just trust me. The more expensive, the better.'

He still does not understand but he tells me that he will. I give him a wink and then walk away.

. . .

BY THE TIME Sheriff Bob finds us another ride back to town, it is almost five o'clock. I ask him to drop me off to see Jessica and Trudy. I want to see them before I head back to the trailer.

I find out where they are by calling Jessica's cell phone and head straight to her parents' house. I call Trudy to give her an update and she tells me that she is packing up to go home. She knew that the sheriff and I made it in time to save Alex. She plans on being home by two o'clock in the morning if she sticks to eighty miles an hour the whole way. I thank her for her help and promise to catch up when Sheila and I get back as well.

SHERIFF BOB DROPS me off outside Jessica's house. I see the lights are on and so her parents must be home as well. I almost reach the steps to the porch when I hear the door open. It is Jessica and she has the door partially closed behind her.

She has changed into casual wear which is a first for me. She is wearing a pair of cute jean shorts and a white hoody. It is the first time I have noticed that her legs have a slight tan. Her hair is tied back in a ponytail leaving her face fully exposed. I see her in a different light and find that in the past week, it seems she has grown up.

I stop in my tracks and wonder who is going to make a move first. I can see in her eyes that she sees me differently. It is the same stare that she gave me when she made a pass at me in the trailer within two days of knowing each other.

Before I make the first move, she quickly rushes down the steps and flings herself at me. I briefly try to push her away from me but realise that she needs to do this.

Jessica kisses me passionately, which I did not see coming. I am too stunned to pull away and feel guilty immediately as I think of Sheila. I wonder how long she needs to get the thought of us out of her system.

Eventually, she pulls away and stares me in the eyes with curiosity. 'I needed to do that. I know I will never see you again. I wanted to make it clear that I fancied you from the moment you came into my newspaper office. I didn't want to regret not kissing you. I know I will be embarrassed tomorrow, but you will be gone.'

I have no words to say and so watch her smile at me and kiss me gently on the lips again. I then watch her walk away slowly like a teenager coming home from her first date.

I WALK AWAY from her house in my own time and once I am far away from her house, I phone Sheila for a lift.

29

TIME TO SAY GOODBYE

Tuesday Day 8 Homeward bound

I WAKE up with my eyes still closed and I forget that we are in a trailer park and not lying in our own bed back at home.

Last night had to be the best sleep I've had since I arrived. A huge weight had been lifted from my shoulders and I could finally sleep without unanswered questions floating in my head.

I open my eyes to see Sheila asleep next to me, lying on her front. She wakes and I smile at her, gazing into her welcoming eyes.

After an hour of talking about my week here and how much of an effort she made, we eventually get out of bed and shower together.

WE HAVE coffee while discussing how our day will go. I tell Sheila that there are a few things that I want to do before we leave.

She asks what they are, and I mention having brunch before we leave, making a stop to see the sheriff, and eventually, meeting Daniel's parents. I want to tell them exactly what happened to their child and how he helped us to find his killers. My wife agrees with me and so we get ready to pack our things and make our stops.

We decide to see the sheriff first, go for brunch about eleven o'clock and then head to the Harris's. We aim to leave Marion by one o'clock.

. . .

WHEN WE HAVE FINISHED PACKING our suitcases, I realise that I still have my crazy wall that helped keep my mind focused. I realise I do not need it anymore and slowly tear down the newspaper articles, witness statements and theories.

I put the information back in the box in its original state. I will hand back the box to the sheriff when I say my goodbyes.

As we leave the trailer park, I take one last long look at my temporary home. I think about what work I did with Jessica and Trudy here. I think about Jessica's reaction when she saw me last night. I wonder if I will ever tell Sheila that I was the crush of a girl in her twenties.

WE LOAD the car up with our things and notice the hire car has already been collected. They must have taken it while we were still asleep.

The site manager, Justine Brown, makes an effort to come and see us off. She appears sheepish and I guess she feels embarrassed about what happened two nights ago when she barged in on us. Sheila and I find it funny and do not make her feel any worse than she already does.

She smiles awkwardly at us and hopes we had a pleasant stay. I go to pay her cash for my stay here, but she will not accept it.

Justine seems to be at peace. 'No. That is on the house.'

I feel awkward not paying my way, so I insist, 'Take it. It was paid for by someone else.'

Justine has a twinkle in her eye as she says, 'You helped this town to heal. That is something I will be grateful for, for eternity. You take care of yourself and drive home safely.'

She unexpectedly hugs me and sniffles as she fights back a tear. I now understand and thank her for her appreciation of my work.

Sheila goes to hug Justine as well and then we finally head off.

We drive slowly out of the trailer park and savour our time here. It feels sad that we are leaving this small quaint town. I think Sheila is sad to leave even though she has only been here for two days.

SHEILA DRIVES us as she feels that I am too exhausted to make the drive back home. When we reach the police station, everyone in the office is pleased to see us. Everyone is friendlier towards us after what Trudy, Jessica, Sheila and I accomplished.

Sheriff Bob hears the commotion and pokes his head out of his office. He waves us over to come in and chat.

I hand over the box to him. 'Here. I won't be needing this anymore.'

Sheriff Bob smiles and chortles a little. 'We won't be needing this anymore ourselves. With the new findings, they will be going away for a long time. Are you heading out now?'

'We going to have an early lunch and then head over to Daniel's parents' house. Explain what a great help he was even to the end. We aim to leave by one o'clock.'

Sheriff Bob appears sad himself. 'We are going to miss you. We will see you again?'

I think about it then assure him, 'Definitely. Thanks for everything, especially your help.'

Sheriff Bob realises that he has not been formally introduced to my wife. 'You are his wife. I apologise for not introducing myself. Everything's happened so fast since you arrived. It only took you one day to help complete the case. And you are off already.'

Sheila laughs at his comment. 'From what I saw, it is nice a town. We will definitely come back.'

Sheriff Bob makes a point of shaking hands with us both again. We only stay for another few minutes before leaving.

WE ARE NOW in the car going for our brunch. I suggest we head to a great breakfast place called 'Crook Door Coffee House' that I first went to. I tell my wife how good their coffee is and that they have a wide selection of food.

Sheila is sold on the coffee and accepts the decision to go there.

WHEN WE ARRIVE at the coffee house, I sense the staff are staring at me differently and one of them is keen to approach us. She is a young woman in her twenties with long curly hair and an enthusiastic smile. She asks if we are okay to sit at the table beside us. I allow Sheila to decide, and she says it is fine.

We sit by the side of the wall, opposite the window and the waitress asks what we would like to drink. We both ask for coffee and ask if she will give us a few minutes to decide on breakfast.

I already know what I want but I still peruse the menu. 'What are you going to have?'

Sheila hums to herself. 'I can't decide. I think I will go for the waffle.'

The same waitress comes back and takes our order and smiles at me again with a sheepish expression.

Sheila kicks me under the table and smiles at me. I pretend she did not do that and give her my order.

Sheila only now notices that the staff are whispering and smiling in our direction. I do not worry about it.

Our food arrives after about five minutes and there seems to be slightly more than I remember. Sheila thinks that these are normal portions.

Out of the blue, I say, 'I have been wondering about what I am going to say to Daniel's parents.'

Sheila is practical and advises me, 'Speak from the heart. That is all you can do. Don't tell them what you think they want to hear.'

I finish eating and say, 'I will consider that.'

After we finish our breakfast, the same waitress again makes sure she comes over to clear our table. I ask for the bill at the same time. She smiles at me again and does not acknowledge my request for the bill.

After she walks away with our empty plates and coffee cups, I leave it for a while before walking up to the till.

When I reach the till, I take out my card. 'We were on that table over there.'

A man, who appears to be the owner, is standing at the till. 'That won't be necessary,' he says.

I do not know if I have heard right so I repeat, 'Here you go.'

The man with grey hair repeats himself, 'That won't be necessary. That's on the house for finding the boy and finding the real killer.'

I cannot accept that, so I insist, 'I like to pay my way.'

The man puts his hand out. 'No. On behalf of my staff, thanks for giving the town closure. Have a safe journey home.'

I guess I have to accept his gesture and thank him. When Sheila and I are about to leave the restaurant, we hear gradual clapping behind us. The sound is quiet at first and gradually gets louder as more join in. We turn round wondering why they are clapping and realise it is for us. I feel embarrassed as I only did my job. I acknowledge them all before leaving.

WE ARRIVE in Yancey Road soon after eleven o'clock and the street is quiet. I try to remember what number they live at. Sheila drives slowly so we can focus on the house numbers. Eventually, we find their house and we park outside next to the sidewalk.

I suddenly have butterflies in my stomach regarding what we will face inside the house. Sheila thought I would go by myself, but I want her by my side for moral support.

I take a take moment before getting out of the car.

WE HOLD hands as we walk up to the front door. I do not even know if they will be home. The street is quiet and leafy.

As we approach the red front door, it unexpectantly opens and we see a woman appear from behind the door.

.   .   .

THE WOMAN HAS LONG grey hair that falls down to her shoulder and she appears, understandably, to have aged beyond her years. She has thin lips with an ashen skin complexion. She has a slim frame and appears frail.

It would seem that she has been expecting us to come and see her at some point. She widens the door to allow us to walk in.

SHE WALKS us to her living room where Sheila and I take a seat on her three-seater floral sofa. I hold my wife's hand while I wait for her to take a seat in an armchair to our right.

I do not know her name as I chose not to learn about Daniel's parents, so, I address her as Mrs Harris.

Mrs Harris is anxious. 'My husband is working today. I assume you are here to tell me how my son was...was...murdered.'

I let go of my wife's hand and lean forward. 'No. I have not come here to tell you how he died. I have come here to tell you how he lived. And what he would have become if his life had not been cut short.'

Mrs Harris sheds a tear.

I tell her a story; 'Daniel would have finished school and realise he wanted to be a cop. He would have decided to go to college to study law before joining the police force. His drive and ambition would have risen him up the ranks to detective. Eventually, he would have been the next sheriff of this town. He would have been a brilliant cop. I know this because despite knowing that he would not make it alive, he left a clue on his hand. That led to a black book that he kept on him all the time. He managed to write the names of his assailants among the chaos.'

Mrs Harris has comfort and closure. 'Would you like some tea?'

We stay for two hours with her husband finishing work early to meet us. They show their appreciation of our work and for finding their sons body for them to lay to rest.

When we have answered all their questions, Sheila and I are ready to head home.

WHEN WE ARE BACK in the car, we stare at each other and gently smile. Sheila asks if we are going to see Jessica as she has spent the best part of the time with us. I go quiet and admit to saying goodbye to her last night. I almost tell her that she has a crush on me and that she kissed me, twice. But I bite my tongue and suggest heading back. Sheila starts the car, and we slowly drive away.

We notice that we will need gas, and both remember that there is a petrol station on the way out.

.   .   .

As we drive into the service station, the same old man comes out to greet us. We stay in the car and the man fills the car up for us.

The old man smiles at us. 'Did you find what you were looking for?'

I smile at him, almost chortling, and say 'Yeah.'

The old man continues to smile. 'Well, that is what is important. I hear you found the boy and who killed him.'

I nod my head, 'Yeah.'

It is not long before we are filled with gas, enough to get us back to New Jersey.

I turn to Sheila and say, 'It is time to head home.'

The man says, 'Thank you for solving an unsolved crime. The people here are grateful.'

He holds out his hand and I shake it before driving away.

The journey feels tranquil as we drive through country lanes before reaching the highway. Somehow, I will miss this place and the oddity of the town folk. I will also miss Jessica but not the part where she tried to come on to me.

30

THE PENNY DROPS

A couple of weeks have passed. As I predicted, there have been nationwide reports on the forty-year-old unsolved case of the missing boy.

I had a few reporters wanting to hear my side of events of how the boy had been found. I refrained from taking my fifteen minutes of fame in the media spotlight.

Even though I gave no interviews, the press still managed to find information about me and went ahead anyway. However, it helped with the sale of the books that I had written a couple of years back. So, I did not do badly from the publicity.

It is a Monday morning with the sun beaming into our bedroom. Sheila and I are lying next to each other, dreading going to work.

I have my second attempt at my interview at the depot which is at ten o'clock and Sheila is leaving for work after nine.

It is quiet with the kids nowhere to be heard. I have the urge to have sex and Sheila has the same idea. We quickly go to make love and as we begin to enjoy our moment, our two kids rush in wanting to show us a newspaper article. That is our sex session scuppered.

Josh and William are both shouting for us to read a report written about me. I roll my eyes and crash my head into the pillow. Eventually, I go to read the paper to shut them up.

All three ask me to read the story aloud. As I read it, I notice there is a picture of Jessica next to the column of text.

It broadly says that I and two intelligent investigative women helped solve a mystery that had plagued a small town called Marion. She mentions briefly how we pieced together the number of incidents that surrounded the disappearance of the boy. Jessica finishes the writing by thanking me for her break into serious journalism. She says her new career in New York City, working for the 'New York Tribunal' where she is thriving, is all down to me.

I guess she now realises what I meant about being the only person to officially report the now-closed case. I knew that the story would be a nationwide sensation, simply because it involved a senator getting behind the idea of freeing an innocent man.

WE ARE all sat around the family table having breakfast together before we leave to do our own things. We have not done this in a long time, and it feels nice. I observe the children laughing and making jovial conversation with their mother. I sit back with a glass of orange juice, enjoying the atmosphere.

It is not long before Sheila realises the time and has to go now. She gives me a peck on the lips and dashes out.

The kids do the same, needing to head back to university, leaving me at home.

I ARRIVE in the car park at about quarter to ten and wait in the car. I mull over what questions might be asked and how I will answer them.

I really do not need the money but need a reason to get out of the house. It can be lonely being home all day with nothing to do.

When it is time to go in, I begin to remember how the interview went last time. It feels strange as I walk back into the shop and walk up to a member of staff. The person is different from last time, and he takes me to the office.

A young girl comes out of the interview room; she looks like she is a college student wanting to find beer money. The same man who interviewed me last time remembers me, and he appears keen to have me in his office. I remember his name is Frank.

HE ASKS me to sit down as he walks around his desk and takes a seat. This interview feels different, like I am a friend he has not seen in years.

Frank smiles at me enthusiastically before saying, 'I'm just going to ask a few questions. You can then ask me any questions you may like. Because I interviewed briefly before, this will be quite quick.'

I sit upright against the back of the chair to acknowledge my understanding. 'No problem. Fire away.'

Frank chortles. 'Funny. A good joke. Now, what are your weaknesses?'

I think of something interesting to say. 'Well, I can be a bit methodical which can make me slow. But it helps me to learn the job faster.'

Frank continues to smile broadly. 'That's a good one. Why do you want to work here?'

I find the question hard as I do not want to be here. 'Well, when I come here to shop, I always find the staff friendly. The customers are nice...'

Frank stops me in my tracks. 'Let's cut the bull s—t. What was it like solving that case that was nearly forty years old?'

I struggle to change my frame of mind. 'It was like any other case. Nothing special.'

Frank is still curious, 'You've got the job, by the way. I just want to hear it from your perspective.'

I have never been asked to discuss a case when being interview in the police force, but I carry on, 'Well, there were holes in the original conclusion to the arrest of the accused. I methodically dissected the original reports and started a new line of enquiry.'

Frank thinks that I am being modest and pushes me; 'You can tell me how great it felt. Bringing the men to justice.'

I choose to use a metaphor to describe the feeling; 'There is a story I once heard. It happened to be a job interview question. You will see where I am coming from. A man is driving towards a bus stop and as he goes to drive by, he sees three people waiting for the bus. The three people are an old woman, who is frail and looks as if she is about to die, an old friend who once saved your life and the third is the perfect soulmate for you. You drive a very small car that can only fit one other person in. Which one would you choose?'

Frank has a puzzled expression. 'It's obvious. I would take the old woman who looks like she is dying and take her to the hospital.'

I smile and explain the answer; 'Exactly. You do not give it a second thought. You do not look around for applause. But you could have given your car to the friend who saved your life. That friend can then take the old lady to the hospital. You would then have the person who is your soulmate. But you didn't think of yourself when applying the logic. That is what it is like to solve a case. You do not do it for something you can gain from it.'

Frank notices me go quiet. 'What is it?'

I find myself solving the final puzzle. 'There is somewhere I need to be. I can start tomorrow. Thanks. You have just help me solve another case.'

With that, I rush off and head downtown.

I END up driving to the leafy part of Washington, to Senator Charleston's house. I have already rung the doorbell and stand there with my back to the door. I admire the flowers along the wall that blocks the view of the road.

A few seconds later, I hear the door open and casually turn round. A maid has answered, and I ask to see the senator. She is an old lady who appears to be retirement age. I did not meet her when I last came here. She is happy to walk me to him without checking my credentials or why I have come.

The maid takes me through the house to the back garden.

SENATOR CHARLESTON IS SAT by himself in front of a white iron flowery garden table. He is having tea while staring out at his huge garden.

He seems to have been expecting me as he asks me to take a seat and drink with him. I politely decline as I sit in the chair next to him, on the other side of the round table.

Senator Charleston seems sad, and I feel that he wants to unburden something. 'I wondered when you would come to visit me.'

I have a theory that I want to run by him; 'Trust me. I did not envisage myself being here today. I had a job interview.'

Senator Charleston chortles, 'I bet. Now you're famous, you can have any job you want.'

I quickly correct him; 'It is only a depot job. The same job I applied for before you had three cop cars ambush me.'

Senator Charleston quietly laughs. 'I remember. Sorry about that. What do you want to know?'

I want to tell him an idea, 'I am going to tell you a little story. You tell me if I am going off on a tangent. I was hoping it would just be the two of us.'

Senator Charleston turns to me and says, 'Whatever you are about the say, you will be correct.'

I think carefully about what I am going to say. 'When I had my interview, I was asked how it felt to solve the most famous mystery. I thought the best way was to tell a story about three people at a bus stop.'

Senator Charleston knows the story and says, 'Yes. The best friend takes the old lady. He gets the girl of his dreams.'

I smile briefly at his knowledge then continue, 'Well, the common answer is to take the woman. Sacrifice your chance of finding true love. The bit 'sacrifice' stuck in my head.'

Senator Charleston can see in my eyes that I have broken wide open another case. 'I know what you are going to say.'

I make it clear that I will explain what I now know. 'There was something that puzzled me - why you strongly believed that Alex Jefferson was innocent. Also, I couldn't understand why a man like him with a promising career would not give up his source to prove his innocence. The part I did eventually work out was his long-suffering secret in his personal life. The penny dropped when he finally left prison; he did not have a look of relief, but sadness. He wanted to go to prison for a separate crime. Something that he would have confided in you. I suspect it was accidental killing. Something that involved a wife. The guilt consumed him, and he felt that the crime he did not commit was his punishment. But, at the same time, he couldn't live with the fact that he was gay.'

Senator Charleston chortles to himself with the knowledge that I am spot on. 'That is why I hired you. Alex was married and his wife killed herself. One day, she came home, and she saw her husband with the neighbour. Nothing actually happened, but she knew. She had the strength to confront him. When Alex confessed, she bought a gun and killed herself. That weighed on his conscience. He felt that God was punishing him. Go on.'

I find this part hard to say aloud; 'Alex Jefferson could not have killed the boy. It was impossible. The reason why I know this is because you two were lovers. An up-and-coming politician. A rich farmer. A loyal wife and grown-up children who have flown the coop. At some point years later, the guilt could not be kept to yourself and so you told your wife. I assume last year. It was her idea to prove his innocence without implicating you.'

Senator Charleston begins to tear up. 'He was my first and only. We had a lot in common and before we knew it, we realised there was something there. Could you imagine back then, especially white man with black man. They would have killed him let alone giving him a life sentence.'

I completely understand. 'Well, you have a choice: Let the guilt consume you so you kill yourself, or you risk going to jail for perverting the course of justice, allowing an innocent man to go to jail. Either way, you answer to God.'

Senator Charleston breaks down in floods of tears. I have my conclusion and leave him to console himself. I leave his house after finally having the last piece of the puzzle resolved. It does not bring me joy.

A FEW DAYS LATER, when I am at home after a day's work at the depot, I read in the paper that Senator Charleston has stood down from his position. There is no mention of his reason and only his wife and I know the reason.

There is a rumour that Alex Jefferson will receive compensation for his wrongful imprisonment in the amount of $8,000,000.

I imagine that Charleston will one day face Alex Jefferson and make up for his loss.

PLEASE LEAVE A REVIEW!

Jane Knight Rogue Officer

Thank you so much for buying and reading my book!!

This is my tenth book that I spent a year writing. I have drawn from my own experiences to create my characters. They are not based on friends or family of real persons; apart from myself and fictional plot.

I mulled over the idea of writing my first novel in August 2016. I then found the courage to begin my first novel in December 2016. I did not finish my novel until March 2018. My wife and I became a family in June 2017. This postponed completing my first novel.

My first genuine review for this book was not until May 2020. I value my readers reviews because I then know they completed my book. Not half completed and never picked up again.

I plan on becoming a full time author by building up my catalogue of various genres that focus on soft erotic themes whether Romance, Action & Adventure or Thrillers.

BOOKS ALSO BY LEON M A EDWARDS

Jane Knight Rogue Officer Book 1
    Jane Knight Fair Game Book 2
    Jane Knight A Spy Among Us Book 3
    Jane Knight Tomorrow's World Book 4
    Blind Love
    Eternity Wing A Pray
    To The Stars
    Ponta Delgada A Good Place To Die
    By Chance

Please visit the following links to these books

Leon M A Edwards Amazon Author Page

Leon M A Edwards Author Website

LEON M A EDWARDS CLUB

Join my Leon M A Edwards Club to receive future free ebook copies before release date.

I like to send out my books before I publish to hear from my readers.

Subscribe

The link above will take you to the subscription page.

Published by Thriller and Intense Limited

www.leonmaedwards.com

Printed in Great Britain
by Amazon

29844106R00106